JOURNEY OF LOVE

Flight 2806 from L.A. to Hong Kong was being prepped for take off. For Max and Dori, California residents who lived only a few blocks from each other but never met, the wheels of fate and destiny were about to put their paths on the most unexpected journey they could ever imagine.

FRED ALAN ROBBINS

For Henry and Sadie Robbins, my parents and most ardent
supporters of all my creative efforts and adventures throughout
my life. I hope they have a good view from up above.

For my brother Steve, who read pages and provided me with
constant positive feedback. And my brother Barry, who
created a beautiful display at his restaurant in Del Mar Ca.,
Milton's, where he proudly sells Journey of Love.

To my friend Brad Campbell, who not only called to ask me
when my book would be available so he could be the first to
buy it, but read my very first pages and kept on me so it was
not written in all three tenses.

And to my long time friend Fred Cobar, who worked tirelessly
in every way possible to get this book published. Without his
creative input, this book would still be a work in progress.

*A glossary of some of my favorite restaurants
and places to heal is located at the end of my story.*

CHAPTER ONE

LEAVING LOS ANGELES

From where Max was sitting, the lush valley floor beneath Mount Batur looked a lot farther than the twelve hundred feet it was said to be. But, make no mistake. If he jumped, he would be dead long before he hit bottom. So, he sat still, and waited. There was no rush. He was living alone, and if he was going to die alone, what difference did it make when it happened? He was waiting for an answer.

He had heard and read about all the theories espoused by religious leaders and spiritual guides. Suicide was not healthy for the soul. It could result in being stuck in what is called *limbo*, living between worlds floating around aimlessly as some form of higher power punishment. A happy, natural death, on the other hand, could have one's soul quickly placed in a new body ready to begin again. This was surely something to consider if a particular person believed in such things.

With this thought and many others racing through his mind, he figured that if he was going to end his life, he might as well do it in his favorite place on earth, Ubud, Bali. It was with this tiny bit of irony, that he was on his way to this little island in Southeast Asia known as the Island of the Gods.

It was in this slice of heaven on earth he would call it quits. It was where he would put the hashtag and exclamation mark on his life, right up to the very end of it. Fifty years of eating well, playing hard, and experiencing all the love and loss he felt he could handle, or live with as was now the case. All he had to do to set this in motion, was get out of the Uber when it stopped at the international terminal for China Airlines at the Los Angeles International Airport.

Like most people who had been through the past two years of our Covid 19 world, Max seemed to have survived the full range of pandemic mania. He made it through all the phases, from the pandemic lockdowns, to the masks and social distancing craziness, and lastly, the vaccination/booster hysteria.

He survived by taking house and pet sitting jobs within the borders of the United States once travel was back on the table and people could get out of their homes again. It allowed him to be more mobile than most, while at the same time being able to avoid crowds. He lived alone in beautiful homes for weeks at a time, his only companions the sweet dogs and cats he was charged with taking care of.

Although he had been to Los Angeles International Airport many times before, this time felt different. He knew he was starting a journey that he was at best uneasy with, and for sure uncertain about. With each step closer to the boarding gate, the knot in his stomach grew a bit tighter. It had nothing to do with Bali, of course. He loved being there more than anywhere else. It was where he called home. He hoped that being in Bali he could turn things around and let that natural happiness and positive energy inside him turn the corner on this dark wave. He was on this flight, this *journey of love*, because he had come to a time in his life where he was no longer sure he was happy enough to keep on going.

He couldn't stop feeling that he was at the end of the road. He was making the only decision he felt he could make. Without a woman in his life to make love to, come home to and laugh with each day, he decided he had enough. He was open to miracles, of course.

Max had been to Bali four other times. On each successive stay, his trips became longer. First by a week, second by three weeks and third by nine months. He was almost a citizen. He had his fiftieth birthday on his most recent trip and learned that his birthday, Aug 17th, was Indonesian Independence Day. That was no coincidence, and he immediately concluded that his life and destiny was in Bali. Call it a sign if you want. He did. It was a natural evolution of all his combined efforts that led him on this final quest to find the peace and harmony in his life that he so desired.

He loved Bali and the slowness of life there. You don't rush Bali. Bali has its own style, its own pace, and high-strung Americans who demand all tasks be carried out in the blink of an eye don't do very well there.

His life was his own now. His parents passed away a few years ago and his total family was his two brothers in San Diego and a couple of very close friends in and around Los Angeles. That was it. If he stayed in Los Angeles, he would have to work to live. In Bali, he could live and the only work he needed to do was on himself. For him, It was an easy choice.

As Max made his way to his gate, he thought about his very first trip to Bali. In the beginning, it was just an idea in his head that had been brewing for a while. He laughed a bit at himself as he remembered what his first trip was like. He was a typical tourist. There were the customary day trips to places like the fabled Monkey Forest in Ubud, the electric bike caravans to see the Tegalalang Rice Terraces, and the most fun and arduous of all, the 2:00. A.M hike up Mount Batur, the holy mountain with the volcano by the same name, for a sunrise you would write home about. Or, post to Instagram.

Max thought about these and so many other life changing events that happened over the course of time as he made his way almost robotically to his gate, shielded from his reality by the throng of anonymous passengers coming and going from all over the world.

He wasn't sure if he wanted to live or die, dance or cry. Life had caught up to him and now it was time to pay the piper as they say. How he would pay was yet to be determined. He lived his life fast and loose, getting by on street smarts and a quick smile. He was the kid on the street corners of Chicago selling cheap watches on one hand and Lady Cornelia Ovenware sets that he stored in the back of a rented van. He always had to hope he wasn't trying to sell the same person twice.

That was a long time ago. A lifetime ago, so to speak. There were no more rented vans to pull into dark alleys for quick sales. No more knock off watches to hide under an extra large, long sleeve shirt. That time had come and gone. He was almost a real senior, not a senior in high school. He had no excuses for being in the situation he was in, alone and afraid and wondering how much longer he could pull off this movie he was staring in.

Max was lucky right out of the gate. His parents provided every opportunity for success any child could hope for. Not in terms of money, necessarily, but with love and support. He realized later in life, that his parents often skipped breakfast at the corner diner so they could bring him his favorite sports magazine and a chocolate donut before the school bus came. The school bus was his dad, of course, who picked up six other kids for the ride to the hallowed halls of Von Steuben High.

There was never a teacher his mother Sadie would not walk to the school to lecture about being unkind to her son. Even if he was caught red-handed throwing spitballs at the blackboard. Just ask Ms. Blanche Prichard. Unfortunately, for his two brothers who would attend the same middle school, he left an indelible mark that put them under extra scrutiny. He was the first born, the black sheep and a perpetual challenge any first time parent might wish to avoid. Yet with all that, the last words his mother said to him were "Do you have everything you need?" How blessed could a son be?

His dad Henry, worked his ass off to keep food on the table and still take his three sons to an occasional White Sox game at the old Comisky Park or to the local playground on a Sunday for a game of catch and to bat a few balls around. He loved the Chicago White Sox, because that was their hometown. For some reason, his three sons were all rabid Yankee fans. Henry understood.

Max knew how lucky he was later in life than his dad might have hoped for, but patience is a virtue and has its own rewards. When his dad was in those final days of hospice care at his home, he mostly slept and was surrounded by his wife and two of his three sons. Thankfully, he heard the words he longed to hear and knew he didn't say often enough himself.

As fate would have it, he had just come home from a great yoga class and when he answered his ringing phone, it was his mom sitting bedside next to his dad. She called whenever her husband of sixty five years was awake enough to say hi. "Just a minute, Max, your father is awake." She passed the phone to him, "Hey dad," Max said loud enough for him to hear.

"I love you," his dad said in barely a whisper. "I love you back," Max said. The words just came out. Two hours of yoga had him in just the right place emotionally for this moment. And, with those words, he heard his dad say, "he loves me back" as he passed the phone to his wife. These are words Max will never forget for so many reasons. But most important, he knew his father knew he loved him. That was a big weight to let go of.

Trying to find answers to his questions, Max would wonder if maybe things came too easy to him. He was funny and smart and with the wisdom of age, he knew he took for granted the few wonderful women in his life who loved him enough to put up with him. If only he could have a do over in that department, he would tell himself.

As he moved towards the gate, his steps were casual. His faded brown leather Birkenstock sandals carried his weight effortlessly. They were expensive and worth every penny. Max was not extravagant in his spending habits, but he firmly believed in getting the best where it mattered most. Good shoes, good phone, good TV when he had one, and a really good mattress.

He finally reached the big departure and arrival flight screen. He stopped to adjust his reversible black and green Prada backpack over his shoulders. It was a gift from his brother, and he loved it. It was the perfect computer bag, light weight and well insulated. And it felt good on his shoulders.

Max opened his phone to his e-ticket boarding pass to double check one last time that everything was going as planned. So far, so good. No changes. He proceeded to his gate, his heart beating just a little bit faster. When his boarding section was called, he placed his phone under the red light manned by the gate agent, and began that long slow walk down the ramp to the aircraft: Boeing's new wide- body 747-8 with a seating capacity of up to six hundred souls.

He made his way slowly, hoping to be seated in a row of very mellow, sleepy people. No non stop talkers would be a gift. The struggle to be quiet and mind his own business was right there in front of him as he watched and waited while people seemed overwhelmed with the simple task of putting carry ons in the overhead bins and getting settled into their seats.

He chose an aisle seat, 22C, so he wouldn't have to crawl over anyone to get to the bathroom. Snug in his seat, earphones on and his favorite yoga mantras playing, he was finally ready for the thrust of the engines that would carry the plane upwards towards into the sky leveling off at forty thousand feet. No turning back now.

CHAPTER TWO

IN THE AIR

Max fished out his writing tablet, a beautiful handcrafted journal he had purchased from his favorite gift shop located in the lobby of Udaya Spa on Sri Waderi street. Getting out his journal brought back fond memories of his days there trying new ways to experience the art of coffee in Bali while writing a story or poem he hoped to publish.

He finally put pen to paper, completely removed mentally, from the long line of passengers still filing in past him. He began what he hoped would be a cleansing of sorts, a cathartic process of writing to his few friends that he would be living in Bali permanently, and that he might not see them again unless they came to visit. He wanted to tell them how thankful he was that they were all part of his life's journey. He was in a groove, letting his feelings out. He barely noticed a group of passengers were bunched together next to his seat and going back a few rows. The flight attendant thought this would be a good time to try and move past everyone to get to the cockpit area.

WHAM—She pushed Dori forward, who landed chest first onto Max's face. Her hands landed hard on each of his thighs as she tried to brace herself.

"Owwww." Max looked up squinting between her breasts. A few passengers were still pushing from the rear, there was a bit of chaos, and he could not see anything, until this noticeably beautiful woman stood up, pulled back away from him and lifted her hands off of his legs. Their eyes locked in a moment of mutual surprise. There were no words to cover this particular situation.

"Hi, Max said sheepishly. You okay?"

"Ummmm…Yeah. I guess so. What about you? I'm sorry I used your legs as my landing spot."

"It's all good, Max replied. I've got about fifteen hours before I have to use them again."

"Funny guy," Dori said with a relieved smile across her face. His clear blue eyes were looking straight ahead at hers and she stayed silent, locked into his peaceful gaze. "You can buy me a drink when they start serving."

Frustrated voices from behind them rang out. "Can we get moving here?" "Get her number, Romeo," another shouted.

Dori kept moving and was happy there was only another few steps. Finally. Three rows back in an aisle seat opposite side of him, 25D, Dori Kominski, a strikingly beautiful woman in her forties of about medium height, long flowing brown hair, and soulful hazel eyes, finished putting her stylish brown and yellow snap tote by Minted, in the overhead bin and settled into her seat. The last bits of that humiliating moment in her history that she will never forget, clung to her like a super glue.

How could this *even* happen she was still asking herself, strapping her seat belt across her waist just a few feet behind this L A yoga guy who just got a full on face plant of one her best features! And he was writing or doodling or whatever, like nothing happened. He didn't even turn around to see where she stopped. Did he even notice that hint of Chanel she was wearing on her skin, she wondered? There is an upside to everything, she hoped. The one positive thing she could put her finger on, was the sweet feeling of butterflies in her tummy.

She plugged her I-Phone into the seat back and selected one of her Spotify tracks from a mediation playlist. She closed her eyes. All embarrassment aside, the first leg of her flight was underway. She had more embarrassing moments in her life, but still, this one was way up there in the top few. She was on her way to a highly sought after yoga teacher training program in Chiang Mai, Thailand. No time for distractions, she thought.

With her eyes closed and her favorite mix playing, she hoped to slip into that higher consciousness she truly loved. She chanted AUM to herself and concentrated on her third eye chakra, but her conscious mind would not let go of the thoughts about the man three rows up and to her left, and the fact that his face was between her beautiful, tan breasts in all their glory for far too long. Being a stranger and all…The perils of a loose V-neck T-shirt she mused. She took one last look in Max's direction. His head was down, fully focused on whatever he was doing.

Did he really not notice the Chanel? Why did she even care was a better question? Maybe it was the black mala beads around his neck, or the multi-colored crystal bracelets that adorned his wrists. It could even be the long white hair that hung freely over his collar or the tanned bare feet resting underneath his knees as he sat in perfect sukhasana, otherwise known as easy pose or full lotus. Whatever it was, she was interested. He was cute, funny and obviously into yoga.

The flight was smooth and easy and the food service was about to begin. Dori had already enjoyed a glass of wine and was feeling adventurous enough to do a "walk by". She timed it perfectly, and just as she neared Max's seat, he heard the squeaky wheels of the food cart and looked up. Whether it was the Universe at work or just dumb luck, when he looked up, Dori was standing next to him in the aisle. There was a flight attendant on one end and the food cart just a few passengers back on the other end. Time to act.

"Hi," Max said, making up for being mostly silent before. He was a social person. As much as he liked spending time alone, he relished talking with someone who either shared his interests or might be open to learning about them. He had the feeling he was on solid ground with Dori. He would find out soon enough.

Dori's smile was sweet, soft, and not too eager. "Hello again. Nice to finally be on the way, eh?"

Max returned the smile. "It sure is. You know you're in for a long haul when you can watch two movies, take a nap, and wake up only to learn it's still ten hours from landing."

"Ha. Don't remind me," Dori replied. I'm trying to forget about the time. "And the day," Max added. "Something to do with the equator. I hope there's no Bermuda Triangle out here."

Dori laughed. She was a good audience. Max liked her and was feeling at ease. "Are you going to Bali," he asked,?

"Thailand for me," Dori replied. "And I think we're safe. I did a lot of research before this trip and no planes have ever disappeared going from Los Angeles to Hong Kong."

"Thank you for such reassuring news," Max replied.

The flight attendant was apparently more interested in trying to place a meal on Max's tray table than helping along a potential romance. She gave them each a slow eye roll and the timeless look of exasperation from someone who has been doing the same thing far too long. She just jumped right in and cut Max off.

"Chicken with vegetables, or fish with jasmine rice," the attendant repeated looking directly at him? And please, Ma'am, can you take your seat during food service?"

"Fish," Max replied, taking the hint. He said goodbye to Dori with his eyes as she stepped around the food cart and moved along on her way to the loo.

"Thank you. Enjoy your meal," the flight attendant answered curtly as she placed Max's tray on his fold down table. She was busy and eager to dispense the hundreds of meals still waiting stacked on her food cart. Food was a drug on long flights. It filled people up and put them to sleep if they had not already taken something from home.

Max noticed the sarcasm, but was more focused on Dori who had resumed her walk down the aisle. He loved the company of women, but since his last heartbreak, and the many years since his last intimate night, he had pretty much put thoughts of romance out of his mind completely. It felt good to meet a beautiful woman and feel the embers burning like they used to.

While Max had his thoughts brewing, Dori was doing her own bit of speculating. Bali, she thought to herself as she walked. Once again, someone she found appealing was on a different path than hers. At least she found out early on. She had her music, movies to browse through and a brochure on the history of the yoga retreat and training program she just spent a nice chunk of her mad money savings on. That would have to do. Her plan was to study yoga and complete a teacher training program. Best to put any thought of romance out her mind and concentrate on the task at hand.

CHAPTER THREE

THE HONG KONG AIRPORT

Four hundred and fifty passengers began the slow process of deplaning into the vastness of the Hong Kong Airport. It was like a small city and deserves its own zip code. Being in the Hong Kong Airport was like being thrust in the middle of the annual four day Lollapalooza concert held in Grant Park of Chicago. Thousands of people walking shoulder to shoulder as far as the eye can see. At least this time, Max was in familiar territory.

Having been to the Hong Kong airport on three previous trips to Bali, he knew exactly where he wanted to go. After a brief check on his final leg of the flight which was about five hours later, he headed to that space between gate 28 and 32 of Terminal Two, to Joe's Coffee and Juice. He found this little gem on his last trip to Bali and loved it.

The coffee was great and it was packed with other American travelers who were looking for something familiar that wasn't a Starbucks, to kill a few hours between flights. As he walked, he remembered his last visit to Joe's on his way back to California. He chatted up a beautiful woman with long blonde hair, Lisa

Brooks, who he was willing to bet a round of drinks with, was from California. The Venice Beach sweatshirt and UCLA running pants made it a pretty sure thing. Was she coming or going was the real question?

The answer came before the coffee arrived and provided a glimmer of hope of something more. She was also headed home to Los Angeles. She and Max had similar itineraries, just different places. Lisa spent a few months at a place he loved, The Yoga Barn. The Yoga Barn was a city of yogis, yogi wannabes and young gorgeous people from around the world. They were tan, fit and limber, wearing only the legal limit of clothing required, and they filled the yoga rooms with sweat and pheromones of love and lust. The long ago Indian Guru, J Krishnamurti, would have loved this place. His philosophy was that the act of sex with a loving partner leading to mutual orgasm was as close to GOD as a person could get. Max agreed and was happy to keep trying for GOD like moments in his life. For him, it was a turn on just being in the room and a sweet torture of the senses he thoroughly enjoyed.

As it turned out, Lisa lived just a few blocks from his Los Angeles apartment. They enjoyed the carefree banter about the places they had each visited and compared favorite restaurants and that sort of thing. And that was it. There was no further connection. But that's not the point. It's the serendipity of it all. That is the magic of life in Bali. A place where serendipity, coincidence and the phrase "meant to be", all just coexisted together peacefully.

Max had some time, and pocket full of Hong Hong dollars from his last trip. He ordered a large, extra hot dark roast latte and an almond butter and jelly sandwich on organic white bread. Way to live it up on a last adventure he thought to himself.

Dori was walking through the same wide and crowded terminal walkways Max had just navigated. She kept looking up at flight boards and gate numbers as she walked, wondering if she would make it to her next flight while at the same time, wondering if she would ever see the man three rows up and to her left who sparked all kinds of thoughts in her mind and even a heart palpitation or two.

She plowed ahead towards the gate that would take her to Chiang Mai, Thailand, eyes darting like a red tailed hawk on the lookout for a field mouse. Her phone rang. It was a welcome distraction. Her best friend, Alison, or Ally as she called her ninety nine percent of the time, was checking in from the home they shared in Los Angeles.

"Hey girl, where the fuck are you?"

"I'm at the airport. Hong Kong, remember?" Dori was so happy to hear her friend's voice, she didn't even take the opportunity to call out her potty mouth. Instead, they both started talking at once, happy to connect and hangout with each other.

"Shhh, Dori said, I have to ask you something, tell you something." And then, while walking, talking and eyeballing every passerby, she saw Max. Or at least she saw the long white hair and bare-feet sitting in easy pose just like the guy who sat like that for nearly fifteen hours on the way to Hong Kong. It had to be him.

"Ok, I need you to listen and then tell me if I am completely nuts, crazy or fill in the blank. I met someone on the flight. I mean, we only talked for a minute or two, but in-between, he got a nice facial of my tits. Now I don't know if I should approach him or just forget about it. He's just ahead of me at a cafe."

"Dori. What the fuck? What are you talking about? You flashed someone on the plane and now you want to have coffee with him?"

"No. I got pushed into him, from behind. I was wearing, well, I still am, that nice bamboo V-Neck, you know- the low cut Shiva Beer design we got on Melrose?"

"Wow. Yes. The one meant for raves and orgies. Nice, Dori."

"Allison. Stop. So, as I was saying, I got pushed and my hands landed hard on his thighs, very close to causing some real damage, and my chest went forward. That was it. Purely accidental and it was over in a blink. He seemed really nice. He acted like nothing happened and then we talked later."

"All I can say, sweetie, is I love you. What are you going to do?"

"I have no idea, Allie. I'm supposed to be thinking about yoga training, spiritual things. You know? Not sex with a stranger. That's so not me."

"Ha. Were you wearing your Chanel," Allie joked?

"Maybe, " Dori said laughing."

"Look. You are totally beautiful. You are sexy and you still have great boobs. And if he didn't notice, then keep on walking. He doesn't deserve you."

"You're funny. And you're sweet, Allie. I'm going to say hello and take my chances. Talk to you later."

"Hey. You think he has a friend there? Man or woman works."

"Good-bye, Allison. Talk to you later. I'm about to place my order. I love you."

As Dori looked at the menu board deciding on what to get, a hand touched her shoulder. It took her by surprise and she jumped a bit as she turned around to see who it was. Ha. Of course, she said to herself. It was 22C. Face plant guy.

In that moment that people say your life flashes before your eyes, she relived that humiliating moment and the accompanying knot in her stomach. It was still embarrassing and she had no time to think and no where to go. He sure didn't act like he was embarrassed or anything else for that matter.

"Hi. I'm sorry if I startled you," Max said as he reintroduced himself to this new woman he found so attractive. "I was coming up for seconds when I saw you get on line. Want to sit and have a drink with me?"

"Coffee sounds great. A friend of mine in Los Angeles told me about this place. I'm glad I found it. Listen… I'm really sorry about before, on the plane. Can I buy you a coffee?"

"Hey forget about it, really. People are nuts these days. I just keep my fingers crossed we can make it from one place to the next without any incidents on board. Honestly, I should be buying you the coffee. That was the best hug I've had in years."

"Glad you liked it. That was second or third date access you got there," Dori said smiling.

"At least we're finally on the ground. Even if we still have some time on our hands."

"I know what you mean. My longest flight before this was from L.A to Asheville, North Carolina. Ever hear of it?"

"I love Asheville, Max said. It's my favorite city in the United States," he added beaming with enthusiasm. This was getting better and better he thought to himself.

"It is pretty cool. I was only there a few days visiting a friend and she was in love with the place. Great beer, great food. It was a live and let live kind of place."

"I know, Max replied. I used to own a home there. If I ever come back to the states, that's where I'll settle. I love small towns. It reminds me of Bali in a lot of ways."

Max could not believe his ears. Was the universe playing tricks on him before he even got to Bali? Who *is* this woman he kept asking himself?

"So let's do this," Dori said enthusiastically. "I'm ready for a steaming hot latte'."

"Cool. I've been here a few times and I actually have a pocket full of Hong Kong dollars I plan on spending. My treat, if that's ok?"

"Sure. Thank you," Dori said with a smile. She was happy she took the chance to say hi to this long haired, beaded stranger. They ordered and sat down at a small table just outside the little kiosk with a throng of other travelers all busy plugging in, charging up, or just simply trying to relax before their next flight.

The hour and minute hands on the wall clock moved ever so closer to their respective departure times and yet they barely noticed. Max had not taken an interest in someone in a long time and it felt really good to talk about his life and hear about hers.

They went on for over a couple of hours, the white noise of mindless airport chit chat the perfect backdrop. Dori got up to use the restroom, and Max used that time to drink his coffee and dig into his food. He was too interested in Dori to bother with either while they were sitting together. When she returned to the table, she saw Max reach into this small shopping bag she noticed on the plane that said Bali Buddha on one side.

"That's a cute bag. What's Bali Buddha, she asked?"

"It's a very cool little organic food and general market in the heart of Ubud Center. It's like a very tiny Trader Joe's. They even have an organic restaurant next door where they put trays of grass under your table for your feet to rest in. Crazy, right?"

"That sounds really nice. Grounding while eating. I want one of those bags."

"Well, I can arrange that. They give these bags to each customer with every two hundred thousand dollar purchase."

"Wow. Only two hundred thousand, huh? It's nice to know I am talking with such a financially stable yogi."

"Well, thank you," Max smiled back. He knew she was kidding, because she did not strike him in any way as a materialistically minded person. Gucci shoes and handbags be damned!

"It's kind of like Monopoly money, Max confided. One million of theirs is only seventy of ours. How is it in Thailand?"

"It's almost the same. One thousand Thai Baht is equal to about thirty three US dollars," Dori replied quickly and proudly.

"It makes living easy, that's for sure, Max added. I decided to make my life much more simple and I don't mind saying I can live like a king and do the things I enjoy every day."

"Like what?" Dori asked.

"Well, I can live with waking up to a gorgeous sunrise and only having to decide if I want to swim first or eat first," Max answered.

"I see you have it all figured out. Good for you," Dori said.

Max wasn't sure if he should have given her any ideas that he could be low on funds and that Bali was one of the few places he could afford to live. It was too late now, and his mind and eyes drifted a bit into space. He was hoping he didn't blow it with this beautiful woman he wanted to get to know.

Dori looked at Max. "Max?"

His eyes were looking at hers but his mind was somewhere else. That was obvious. She touched his arm gently. "You okay?"

"Sorry. Yeah, I'm good. Must be some sort of pre jet lag jet lag." Max knew that was pretty lame, but Dori accepted his reply and carried on. "So, if you don't mind me asking, or think I am being nosy, I couldn't help but notice you were busy writing in your journal most of the flight. Are you writing a novel or a screenplay?"

"I'm writing letters to friends in case I don't see them again." Max pulled out his Bali writing tablet with the letters tucked in-between the front and back covers for a little show and tell.

"Nice journal," Dori said, checking out the cover. "It looks like it's bound to inspire great thoughts. But, forgive me, that does sound a little ominous. Why would you never see them again?"

It was an honest question, but one Max did not want to get into with someone he just met. Especially, when that someone was a beautiful woman he was becoming interested in. "My friends don't travel to far away places. Honestly, I could've moved to Seattle and never seen them again either."

"All right. I'll let you off easy this time, but only because you're paying for the coffee. Actually, it's cool that you like to write letters. It's a lost art these days."

Dori knew that what she said might have been a little uncalled for, but she felt comfortable to be herself. She had been told a few times she could be a little sarcastic when given the opportunity, and what's a little sarcasm between friends or potential friends anyway? Hopefully, nothing, she thought.

"It's all right, Dori. Nothing wrong with a little sarcasm between friends."

Max checked his phone and saw it was fully charged. He unplugged from the port, gathered his things and got up from the table to get his backpack on his shoulders. It wasn't clear if he wanted to avoid any more talk of his letters and his travel plans, or anything personal for that matter. He didn't say much about his true feelings on life these days. This was an intricate dance along the walls of ambiguity.

He was ready for his next flight. Maybe, it was just time to go. Clocks ticking, restless feet shuffling, that sort of thing. Max loved the unpredictability of life in times like this, the fortuitous meetings in the most unlikely of places that had always given him reason to look forward to the next day.

"Dori, I'm really happy to meet you. I have a feeling if I met you in LA, I would have a letter here for you as well. I hope your time in Thailand is amazing."

Max and Dori's reach for a hand shake turned into an extended warm hug when she stood up to say goodbye and exchange happy travel wishes. She even added a sweet kiss on the cheek. "Safe travels, Max. I'm also happy we got to meet and talk. I hope whatever you do in Bali makes you happy."

Max got his backpack on his shoulders, grabbed his Bali Buddha bag with his left hand and walked away. He only got a few feet before he turned around. Dori was still standing there so he raised his voice just a little to make sure she could hear him over the sound of rolling suitcases.

"I'll be at Om Ham Yoga Retreat in Ubud. If you get a break before your classes start, I would be happy to show you around."

"Maybe, Dori replied. It is on my bucket list."   "Cool. You never know, right?" Max said looking directly at her.

With that, Dori smiled and he was on his way. He turned toward his gate, his mind drifting, his body a little tired, as he shifted the backpack on his shoulders trying to even out the weight of it all. He threw the Bali Buddha bag over his left shoulder and padded along. The only thing he could hear now was the sound of wheels spinning in his mind.

Dori walked back to the counter at Joe's to refill her tea and decided to try a bag of crunchy kale granola to carry her through until she landed in Thailand. Enough of the airplane food. When she came back to her table, she saw it. Max left his journal on the side table to his left where his phone was charging. It was now a full blown contest between her mind and stomach for which was churning harder. She stood hopefully, her eyes searching for any sign of him. She moved a few feet to the left and then the right to no avail. She even tried standing on a chair. He was long gone in a sea of backpacks and baseball caps.

CHAPTER FOUR

THE LETTERS

Dori sat comfortably at her gate, 63B to Chiang Mai, her eyes glued to the stack of letters she rescued from inside his journal. She shuffled through them, and placed the one addressed to Laurie, on top. It was an easy choice. The other four letters were addressed to men.

She might as well see what Max had to say to the one woman he deemed important enough for a letter. At least that's how she rationalized it. Was she jealous already, she asked herself? Is Max running away from a broken heart? If so, that's the last thing she needs to dive into as she embarks on her own spiritual journey. Her inner debate did not last long. She pulled letter number one out of its envelope and unfolded it.

Hi Laurie,
If you're reading this, I'm most likely looking
down at you from high above. But don't worry. I
won't be a nuisance. You've done so well with
making your life the wonderful happy life you
are living. I'm really proud of you and I never
had any doubt. Your will power and determination
were inspiring to me and second to none. I loved
you so much for so many reasons you never knew.
I'm thankful you came into my life and stayed as long

as you did. I wanted to say I love you one last time.

Love,
MAX

Dori stopped and folded the letter back into its envelope. She was not sure she wanted to pry any further into such a personal and emotionally raw exchange between two people who obviously had some very deep and complicated feelings for one another. Unsettled feelings she guessed. She also knew, the more she delved into this, the more awkward it could be, would be, when and if she ever met Max again. This was crazy. Probably better to just move on and think of this as one of those fleeting moments in life. A moment in time that allowed for thinking of all the fun possibilities with the safety of knowing you would never see the other person again. Yet, as she was processing these thoughts, her feet were moving towards the gate agent with a mind of their own. When she reached the agent, she saw that her flight was due to depart in only twenty five minutes. Not much time for what she was thinking.

"Something I can help you with, Ma'am," the Chinese agent said in flawless English. The agent was in her crisp, soft grey China Air uniform consisting of a blazer with assorted travel patches and a tight matching skirt. She was the model of professionalism designed to make her country proud and show the world China knows how to do things right.

"I'm not sure," Dori replied, trying to give herself more time to think. "When is the next flight to Bali, and can I exchange my ticket to go there instead?"

The agent, Sun Yu Kim, according to the shiny chrome name tag clipped above her breast pocket, checked Dori's boarding pass, gave her a quizzical look and then scanned her computer screen. "There is a flight to Denpasar, Bali in two hours. You would arrive at 9 P.M I have five seats."

"I'll take one." That was that. Dori's heart spoke before her mind could take over.

CHAPTER FIVE

INTO DENPASAR

Max settled into the short six hour flight into Denpasar. It was short compared to the first leg that was fifteen and a half hours and short for well seasoned travelers who learned to watch a good movie instead of checking the flight path on their video screen. He reclined his seat as far as it would go and his plan was to wake up just as the wheels hit the tarmac in Denpasar. It was a good plan for the most part. All he had to do was close his eyes and let sleep overtake his conscious thoughts.

It was a good idea in theory. But sometimes the subconscious mind wins out whether we like it or not. And so, it was no surprise to him that he was thinking about Dori. He thought about her beautiful smile, her long brown hair and the low cut T-shirt that was the highlight of their first meeting. Now, he wondered if he acted like an aloof asshole or like he wasn't interested in her.

He tried to convince himself it really didn't matter. She was off to Thailand and he was almost back in Ubud, where he planned to see a few people, mail his letters, and then find out if he would be able to follow through with his plan to end this physical life on earth and hope GOD and the Universe would not be so mad at him that he would not get to come back quickly and try again.

He would do things differently if given another chance. It's not that he had regrets. He didn't. He wouldn't let himself get caught up in that dangerous game. Each decision leads to the next and it's a waste of time to think if you did one thing differently, took job A instead of job B, life would be better. All we know for sure, is that life would be different. He would go slow. You don't rush Bali.

His mind was one contradictory thought after another. He never felt happier in his life. He was fit, healthy, generally smiling and laughing, but there was a dark part of his brain that was telling him to give up and check out. With "Har-Har Wahe Guru" by Nirinjan Kaur, one of his favorite mantras playing gently into his earbuds, he finally shut down and drifted into a peaceful, relaxed state of being. Soon, a half smile parted his sleeping lips as he saw himself standing with Dori on a moonlit beach holding her hands in his, looking into her eyes. "You're so beautiful," he said.

Dori leaned into kiss him, and the kiss was erotic and sensual. Max kissed her back gently, then more passionately as he moved his lips from hers and down the side of her neck to the top of her low cut spaghetti strap beach dress. She shrugged her shoulders enough so that the straps fell to their respective sides revealing her beautifully, California tanned breasts. She held her right breast up for Max to kiss and they both eased down to the sand using their clothes for a blanket. Max and Dori, their naked bodies shimmering in the moonlight, moved together as if in tune to the sound of the rolling waves. Their legs perfectly entwined, their hearts beating as one, Max moved his mouth slowly down past Dori's belly button, kissing her thighs, brushing his lips against her sweet opening, kissing all of her. He lingered until he heard her moans and felt her hips move in tune with him. Dori looked lovingly into his eyes. "Max, Max." There was no movement. Then a small hand gently shook his right shoulder.

"Sir, please wake up," the flight attendant was saying as she gently shook him until his eyes opened. We have landed in Denpasar. All the passengers have deplaned."

"Oh, wow. I can't believe it. How long was I sleeping?"

"Not long. But the cleaning crew is here and you must leave. Enjoy your stay in Bali, sir."

"Thank you. Terima Kasih, he repeated in Indonesian. I'm sorry about that."

He really wasn't sorry. That was the best dream he had in a long while and he wondered if it was a new sign. A sign of things to come, or just a sign that his subconscious mind was still capable of giving him a sweet, sexy dream he could escape reality with. Either would be just fine with him. He stood up and reached into the overhead bin for his few things. He grabbed his backpack and Bali Buddha bag and walked off the plane and into Indonesia. He stopped to use the restroom and adjust himself and wash his face before getting into the long line at customs.

It finally dawned on him that his Bali Buddha bag felt really light. He reached down into it with a sense of panic, and sure enough, it was empty except for his sunglasses. Fuck! He looked into that bag three more times thinking somehow he missed it and it was really still there. But, of course, it wasn't. Now what? It was really only letters.

No reason to get all crazy and ruin the mood of a really great dream. There was a reason he was here, and it was not to take a walk through the Monkey Forest Sanctuary or pose for selfies. And he would surely have time to re-write his letters if he wanted to. Maybe he could make them better. Happier. Less morbid. Maybe, he wondered, if he wasn't better off without them.

The airport in Denpasar was a beautiful chaotic mess to his tired eyes. A few thousand people at least, were converging on the slow moving baggage conveyor belts neatly arranged by airlines in alphabetical order. Finally, his black four roller with a long white sock tied snugly around the handle so it would stand out from the rest, inched towards his reach. He grabbed it, and was on his way. Next stop Customs then the sweet, comfortable bed at the Hilton Garden Inn near the airport.

CHAPTER SIX

UBUD BALI

Daylight was a beautiful thing. Max chose the eleven P.M. departure from Los Angeles because it landed in Denpasar at three twenty in the afternoon. By five PM he would be asleep in his suite at the Hilton Garden Inn, barely a mile from the airport. It was a Hilton, but it was a Balinese Hilton, and he loved it. Traffic in Ubud was as bad as any city in America and there was no good reason to spend two hours in a taxi after being on an airplane for twenty one hours and going through customs. Get to the hotel, sleep and have your first of many amazing meals. The next day would come soon enough to get things started.

Max was heaping scoops of freshly scrambled eggs and sides of tropical fruits on a big white plate thinking about the first time he met the tour driver, Wayan Suker, who was now his friend. He met Wayan on his first trip to Bali when he was picked up for a session with one of the most well known healers on the island, Hirokie Rei.

This elderly healer was ninety three years old and still going strong. His hair was long, dark black, and wiry, with a complimentary full length beard that went well past his chin. He could have easily passed as a Rastafarian of fame and fortune. He surely had enough of an entourage for one to assume something like that. He sat on his throne looking out at the crowd who had come to hear his words of wisdom, the foretelling of their futures, and remedies for their aching knees or hearts. It was a different kind of tour adventure and was listed under the spiritual outings section of temple visits and healing type activities that were of particular interest to him.

When Wayan and Max arrived, there were already twenty people sitting in easy pose on the grassy area just below a wooden deck where Hirokie had his altar. His assistants stood behind him out of respect ready to get whatever the old healer asked of them. Thankfully, Wayan brought water and sat with Max and told him some stories about the history of the ancient healer and reminded him to just breathe, relax and wait for his turn. Max did just that, waiting peacefully, listening and enjoying the fortunes and advice the old man gave to the other guests.

There was no private room so if you didn't want to put your troubles out in the open for everyone else to hear, you were in the wrong place. After all was said and done, the most memorable part of the whole thing for him, was when Hirokie grabbed the end of his big toe and squeezed so hard he nearly jumped off the deck. "You are strong for many more years," the old man said before motioning for him to leave the stage and for the next person to come up. "That will be thirty dollars," one of the assistants said to him when he got back down to the grassy area.

Max couldn't help but laugh. Other guests were told long fortunes with promises of love on the way, given remedies for their aching bones with his profound assurance they would be running with no pain in just a few days, and all he got was a pat on the back. Oh, well. It was an interesting experience and he would leave it at that. He was happy enough that the pain in his big toe finally subsided. The best part of the morning was that it was a wonderful beginning to a long friendship with Wayan and it was always a great story to relive.

Max was refilling his coffee cup when he saw Wayan walking in his direction waving hello and smiling. He was in his traditional wardrobe of starched white sarong, white shirt and brown udong that fit snugly on his head. He met Max and sat down with him at his table thankful for the invitation to show up hungry and be his guest for breakfast.

"Hello Mr Max. How are you? So good to see you back in Bali where you are so happy. You stay long time?"

"Selamat pagi, Wayan. It's great to see you as well. I'm not sure how long, but at least a few months. Plenty of time to get to the Holy Water and go see your healer friend Made'."

"Very good, Mr Max. Made' will be happy to see you."

"Perfect. Please, go get some breakfast and tell me what's been going on at home." He watched warmly as his friend went to the buffet table to fill up some plates. Wayan loved to eat and being at a nice hotel with so many dishes to choose from was a rare treat. Max had taken him to eat a few times before and the humble nature of the Balinese people was always on display. He pushed his friend to order what he wanted, not the least expensive thing on the menu. It felt good to be like the rich uncle who visited on Christmas and took the family out to a restaurant they would not usually go to.

Max remembered a few greetings and a friendly "good morning" in the local language was always appreciated. Names were pretty easy to remember. Wayan is the given name of the first born in Bali. It could be a boy or a girl, but first born is often named Wayan. Simple. No name books to go through or time spent thinking of a cool name.

After finishing a great breakfast, Wayan walked out ahead of Max to bring his van to the front doors of the hotel. He was a tour operator and he kept his van sparkling clean and filled with water bottles and small snacks for his guests. When Max got in Wayan reached behind his seat and handed him a plastic bag filled with fruit. "My wife says to give you these mangos from our yard. You are like family to us now, and we hope you will come to join us for dinner on this trip."

Max opened the bag and the sweet aroma of the ripe, organic fruit filled the van from front to back. In pure cave man style, Max took out one of the bright yellow and orange mangos and bit into it enough to peel back the skin and satisfy his taste buds. "MMMMMM. So good. Thank you, Wayan. Please tell your wife thank you. I would love to. I met your son last during my last trip and it would be wonderful to meet the rest of your family. Let's get me over to Om Ham and when I get settled into my routine I will text you to come and get me."

"My wife and daughter will be very happy. So Om Ham for your hotel Mr. Max?"

"Yes, Wayan. I will be there at least a few weeks. But first, take me to the Wooden Spoon. I would like to get some cookies and treats for the staff and my friends. And something for our ride. Is that good?"

"Bagus, Mr. Max. Very good. Now we go." He smiled and cranked the engine on his trusty Toyota cargo van and they were off on the narrow roads of Ubud. The roads were dotted with huge holes from the constant downpours during the rainy season and sometimes it was hard to tell where the road began and the shoulder of the road ended. To the Balinese people, that hardly mattered. They drive and honk their horns on a par with any taxi driver in New York City. The difference being, that they honk to say " hey- I'm coming around the corner" not to say " get the fuck out of my way."

The van came to a stop in the driveway of the Wooden Spoon. Max was happy to get out and stretch his legs. It was a good feeling to be back somewhere familiar, and the thought of stepping into the warm, aromatic bakery brought a much needed smile to his heart.

The smell of freshly baked sourdough loaves wafting through the air and the view of gorgeous chocolate and almond croissants lining the bakery shelves would have you believe you were in a Parisian Patisserie. It has been an interesting journey to this point. This stop was merely icing on the cake so to speak. Meeting Dori, erotic dreams on the plane, and the now familiar sights and sounds of Ubud, Bali had finally set the stage for whatever would happen next.

Max came out of the bakery/restaurant with a big bag of treats and handed a small bag with a chocolate croissant to Wayan. "It's very good to see you, Wayan. I am happy to be in your care once again." "Terimah Kasih Mr Max."

"Sama Sama, Wayan". (You're welcome) This was about the extent of Max's Indonesian vocabulary, but for now, that was all he needed. He was in the company of friends.

As Wayan pulled into the arched driveway of Om Ham, Max felt the same kind of pull in his stomach and heart as a person returning to his High School's Ten Year Reunion to see his first love. Flooded with emotions that ran the full gamut from doubt to ecstasy he grabbed his backpack and walked slowly ahead of Wayan up to the registration desk. There, just like on his second visit one year earlier, his name was spelled out in soft colored chalk on a welcome board-WELCOME BACK MR. MAX.

Underneath his name, were the names of other guests arriving that day. It was a nice touch and Max enjoyed seeing the names of his new neighbors. He also laughed as he remembered how he used to refer to Om Ham when he stayed for so long. Om Home he would say. And he meant it. He never felt more loved and happier anywhere on earth in all his seventy one years.

Om Ham was more of a yoga retreat and spiritual center than a regular hotel, but in terms of being set in the midst of lush green rice fields and a vast array of flora and fauna, it was like most other places in Bali. The landscape everywhere was truly spectacular. At the registration desk, Kadek and Govinda spotted Max getting out of his taxi and came running to get his things and greet him with warm hugs.

"So good to see you again Mr Max. We have prepared your room and have a welcome dinner for you. All the staff are happy you have returned."

"Thank you, Govinda," Max replied. He bowed as he said it with his palms together in prayer pose at the center of his chest. This is a familiar and warm greeting and something everyone can share and feel part of the Balinese culture. Max was right at home in an instant.

CHAPTER SEVEN

DORI TAKES FLIGHT

ori was comfortable in her seat even though her heart was beating much faster than normal. She was on her way to Bali with a stack of letters someone she hardly knew had left behind at the airport. She knew this was one hundred percent crazy, but she also felt one hundred percent right. She was sure of it. With that thought in mind, Dori figured the next thing she should do is at least read one more letter. There was still four more hours of air time to fill. She shuffled through the stack and decided on the one addressed to Cousin Brad.

BRAD

Hey Brad. Sit tight. Or whatever they say
up there. I'm on my way. I can't give you
an exact date, and I know it's selfish of
me to want you to wait around when there
are most likely an abundance of awesome
opportunities for you to begin a new life.
A loving family and all the electronic
gadgets you could ever want, await. But if
you can, I would love a few more adventures.
   Or visit me in Bali if you want. A Moped
ride or two? Remember those days? I'm

writing just in case you are still there
when I arrive- assuming I will arrive near
you. Anyway, I sure miss you. Thanks for
showing me your big smile that one day
during Tibetan Bowl meditation with Lady
Wakuha. I set my intention for you to say hi,
and sure enough, I looked up about twenty
minutes in, and there you were- Big smile,
wavy black hair shooting by me like a ghost:)
I hope I see you again somewhere.

Love, MAX

Dori folded the letter and placed it back inside the journal. Good letter she thought. Much better than reading about the broken heart of a man she would like to get to know. But still, she wondered. Why does he think he will be seeing his cousin in heaven so soon? Does he have a life threatening illness? He seems so fit and happy. She let out a big sigh, and decided there was only one way to find out. Maybe the truth would reveal itself in the remaining letters. She had plenty of time and reached into her purse to grab the next one.

The next few hours passed easily with Dori engulfed in reading and trying to interpret the state of mind of this stranger in her life whose most private thoughts dropped into her lap. She had ten days before her yoga teacher training program started and taking this adventure was something she was not entirely sure she should be doing. But, she was about to land in Denpasar, Bali, so should or should not was too late to be thinking about.

Her intentions were simple. She would look for Max and hand him his letters. He would ask her if she read them, and she did not have an answer for that. Maybe she wouldn't tell him she found the letters. That would leave it up to Max to reveal a little more about who he is and what's going on in his life. And if she was going to get involved with someone, that sounded like a reasonable thing to expect. Of course, she had no idea where he was or a phone number or email to connect with. All she knew was she had an invitation to meet him at Om Ham. That would have to do for now.

There were other choices as well. She could just enjoy being in Bali and explore some of the many points of interest Max had told her about. One stood out to her in particular, and that was meeting a very special village elder Max had raved about in terms of his ability to explain your past and look into your future.

Max mentioned his name was Made' and he is a spiritual healer and herbalist who lives in the same family home for many years with many generations of family members. It is not uncommon, she was told, that in homes like Made's where the men in the family before him were also healers, that's it is customary for the children to follow in the parent's footsteps if they had the calling. Considering Made' was the second most popular name in all of Ubud, Dori had yet another glimpse into this crazy adventure she was on. However it turned out, this was the most spontaneous thing she had ever done, and being in a land where serendipity was as common as a cup of chicken noodle soup in a Jewish Deli, how could she go wrong?

The airport at last. Dori was happy to be off of airplanes and be somewhere new with an adventure at hand. She made her way through the maze of the Denpasar airport keeping focused on all signs that pointed to the customer service and transportation desk Max had told her about. He mentioned there would be hundreds of people all gathered around a big desk in the shape of a semi circle surrounded by people looking in all directions for their own hotel van driver or the drivers holding up signs with their guest's names.

Dori kept her tired feet moving and felt a sigh of relief when she spotted the taxi area. Just another couple hundred feet past that would be the airport parking lot which would be lined with Blue Taxi Service cabs waiting for customers. Dori took a deep breath and pushed past the crowd, into the parking lot and there it was. She waved and said hello to the first driver she saw and in minutes, she was on her way to the Hilton Garden Inn in Denpasar, Bali. She made it.

The airport was a bit hectic, but still, Dori felt it wasn't as bad as Max had led her to believe. You've seen one, you've seen them all she thought. She felt good and now she was ready for the next step in her spontaneous adventure. She took Max's advice about spending the first night at a hotel near the airport and getting a good meal and a good night's sleep.

Max suggested the Hilton Garden Inn and for one night it really didn't pay to look on websites when she had no idea where she was anyway. Done. Hello Hilton. For less than $2.00 and in less than an hour from getting off the plane, she was walking through the entrance way of her first Balinese Hotel. Well, American Balinese Hotel. It was gorgeous. Indonesian tapestries covered the walls, beautiful tiles paved the floors, and Balinese lights hung from the ceiling throughout the lobby. As Dori waited to walk up to the counter to get her room key and sign in, she was greeted by a beautiful young Balinese woman who had a delicious looking drink on a small tray. "Welcome to Bali," she said. Please enjoy.

"Thank you," Dori replied, as she eagerly reached for her drink. She was thirsty and didn't wait for any further encouragement to take a sip. With her drink in one hand and her key in the other, a young man from behind the counter came around to escort Dori to her room. She was happy to have some of the small Indonesian currency Max recommended and when they arrived at room 301, she handed him a fifty thousand dollar note. That was about three dollars and fifty cents American and he was thrilled. That's a big tip to the Balinese people and it goes a long way for the Americans and other tourists who show their generosity. It comes back in spades.

Her room was comfortable and the bed was decorated with small towels in the shape of animals. A monkey towel and a chocolate mint were on her pillow. Dori took a picture of it before unfolding it and stripped down to the beauty and comfort of her bare skin.

Refreshed after a long hot shower, she got under the covers and put her music on, and was ready to let the day go and sink into a good night's sleep. There was however, a thought that kept popping up in her mind while she lay still on the bed. Does she tell Max she found his journal? If she does, she would have to tell him immediately and then work through the fact that she read his letters. There would be no way to interpret how he would react. Enough, she said to herself. Time to sleep.

The dream of a much needed night's sleep was soon drowned out by the five A.M chanting that was coming from a Hindu Temple right behind the hotel that was in close proximity to her room. So much for that, she thought. The drone of long, deep AUM sounds followed by the ringing of bells, was her welcome to Bali. What did she expect, she laughed to herself. The morning drive with Mark and Mark on K-Earth 101? She took a very long, hot shower and slid into a comfortable pair of khaki shorts. A white T-shirt from AROMA CAFE was the top item in her suitcase and she was too tired to dig for anything else.

This was Indonesia. It was either hot, sunny and humid or hot and humid with rain. T-shirt and shorts would have to do. Anyway, she loved Aroma Cafe and was quite sure no one else in Bali would be wearing one similar. A nice pair of open toe sandals and she was ready for breakfast. It was time to find out if the food was as good as Max was bragging about. If it was, she could forgive him for forgetting to mention the free 5.A.M wake up call.

Dori had been to plenty of expensive brunches in Los Angeles and Las Vegas. Las Vegas, especially, with almost endless rows of food and drink to help people forget how much money they lost the night before. But when she made her way into the dining room, she could feel her eyes widen and her mouth watering. The buffet area was not crazy long, but the food items were a very unique experience for her. She was stuck in place simply looking at everything.

It was hard to figure out what to put on her plate first. As if someone was listening to her inner thoughts, help arrived. She was escorted to a table by a beautiful young Balinese girl, definitely no more than nineteen or twenty. Her English was excellent and much appreciated.

One of the things Dori learned on her limited foreign travel, was that the English was always better spoken at name brand American operated hotels. It had to be. The customers coming to a Hilton did not want to order scrambled eggs and get a plate of fish heads on rice. The sarong and cultural attire made Dori feel like she was sitting in a scene from the movie Hotel Mumbai. So many people worked to make sure not even the smallest detail was overlooked.

"Would you like coffee to start, Ms. Dori? I saw your name at the top of the restaurant sign in sheet and so far, it is only you. You are early riser, yes? My name is Putu. Welcome."

"Very nice to meet you, Putu. Yes, my name is Dori. And yes, early riser, but I had help this morning. Is the 5:00 A.M chanting a regular thing?"

"I'm afraid so. There is a big temple on the other side of the hotel. I hope it did not disturb you."

"No, not at all. It was beautiful. Putu is a beautiful name. May I ask what order of birth that is in your family? Today is my first day in Bali, and I was told Wayan is the name for the first born in a Balinese family."

"Yes, Ms. Dori. Wayan is number one born name. Putu can also be for the number one born. You will learn many names while you are here. I am happy to help. Would you like cappuccino, latte, mocha, anything special?"

"A hot cappuccino sounds perfect. Maybe two," Dori said smiling.

"I will be right back. Please get a plate or two and help yourself around the buffet. Everything is delicious."

"Thank you, Putu."

Dori was off to fill her plate with some well recognizable choices like fresh thick cut bacon and scrambled eggs, along with a few Indonesian specialities like Bubur Ketan Hitam, a traditional sweet porridge made with a combination of coconut milk, palm or cane sugar, and black glutinous rice. Fresh picked coconuts with bamboo straws, outrageous fruits of all colors and homemade jams made up just one section of the buffet. While Dori was savoring her porridge, a Balinese server in his starched white Hilton uniform, worn over his traditional clothing, approached Dori's table.

"Is everything to your satisfaction, Ms Dori? My name is Budiarta. I am the manager of the restaurant here."

"Thank you, Budiarta. Everything is so good. I can't believe how much I am eating. This porridge is really amazing."

"So happy you enjoyed your breakfast. A friend of yours told me you might be here for a night and I was hoping it would be on my shift. Mr Max from Los Angeles."

"Max told you I would be here?"

"Yes. Well, he said maybe. And if you did, to be sure and get you a driver for wherever you are going. He mentioned you might want to go to Om Ham. He arrived there yesterday."

"That little stinker."

"What, Ms. Dori? What is stinker?"

"Nothing bad. It's an expression of affection, like when someone you know does something to surprise you." That was the best way she could explain it. American colloquial expressions can take on the meaning of the moment, and at this moment, she meant, the nerve of that guy! While at the same time, she was happy he was her stinker.

"I have known Mr. Max for two years now and he is nice man. I hope you have good time. He makes many nice surprises for his friends here."

"That would be great, Budiarta. Thank you. I will be ready in an hour."

"Terima Kasih, Ms Dori. So nice to see you. Your driver will be at the front registration. Selamat Tinggal." (good afternoon)

Dori took that to mean thank you and goodbye and when she polished off the last bit of purple porridge, she retreated to her room to pack and get ready for day number one. It seemed like her mission to find Max would not require the skills of a Sherlock Holmes.

CHAPTER EIGHT

GETTING SETTLED

Max used his first day at Om Ham to catch up with his friends who were either at Ashram Munivara, which was directly across the street, or at the resort, or both. For people staying at the Ashram, life was a little more spartan. There were dorms with cots and no air conditioning. It was either fresh air from the often blowing winds, or the ceiling fans hung from the wooden rafters. It was also a much deeper spiritual experience in that the yogis who taught and trained there also lived there along with the Guru of the Ashram, Ketut Arsana.

He led many beautiful Balinese ceremonies that were accompanied by the countless blessings he gave to each person attending. Full moon celebrations, seasonal equinox celebrations and other holidays too numerous to mention were always special nights at the ashram. In his full ceremonial attire, Ketut would walk slowly behind each guest, say a prayer and put his hands on their heads gently passing his healing energy to their hearts and souls.

Max thought of the time he purchased his first necklace of prayer or mala beads. They come with 108 beads with one large one in the center and other assorted decorations depending on the price and size. The purpose of the 108 beads is that a person is supposed to roll the beads slowly between his thumb and index finger while saying the prayer Om Namah Shivaya. By the time you repeat it one hundred and eight times, you have forgotten what was bothering you and are usually feeling calm and centered. At least, that's the intent.

So Max picked out a set of black lava beads with a gold colored tassel and took them to the Guru's Master class. He wanted the Guru to bless them but he didn't want to ask him to. He wanted it to just happen naturally. After class, the Guru walks around to each student and gives a short blessing with his hands over the student's head. When the final gong came ending class, Max put his prayer beads on his heart and placed his hands by his side palms facing up in resting pose, or shivasana. When the Guru got to him, he put his hands on Max's head for a moment and then, instinctively, put both his hands on top of Max's heart, covering the beads and whispering a short prayer. Max smiled from deep inside feeling the love of his teacher, and just knowing that all he had to do was trust and his needs will be met. It's a moment of his time in Bali that always makes him smile. He still laughs because as much as he loves his mala beads, he wears them as a necklace far more often than he uses them in prayer.

Ketut Arsana was about eighty years old the last time Max saw him, and his long white beard decorated a very tan and weathered face. He had been teaching and healing people from all over Indonesia for forty years. It is told all around Ubud, that Ketut Arsana is the one who brought kundalini yoga to the island and as he perfected his art and teachings, his healing center, Bodyworks, became the go to place for any physical ailment that needed attention. Max laughed as he thought of first massage with the Master.

He was led up a long flight of cement steps to a small but spiritually decorated healing room with various Om Symbols and photos of the Guru with his teacher and by himself. He got on the table and the first thing the master said to him was, "Mr, Max, it is okay to scream or cry. No one will hear you". Max 's request for a stick to chew on was denied and the healing began. An hour later he was downstairs by the meditation room having a cup of ginger and lemongrass tea and feeling like he had an out of body experience. His mind was free and clear and he could not even decide what to do next. He just sat there for a while watching the fish in the Koi pond.

Max was happy to be back at Om Ham. It was more typical of a resort that offered yoga than the Ashram, but had the same teachers and intensity and was owned and run by the same people. For the additional ten dollars per night, he had the comfort of a twenty four hour registration desk where someone could be reached by phone in case of an emergency. It was a safety net that at his age he felt was important to have.

He also appreciated the great air conditioning, the tv's, the full service restaurant and a wonderful healing pool that you never had to dip your toe into first to test the water. You could just dive right in and be so happy you did. The pool was said to have magical healing powers as it was built by hand by the Guru. He blessed every rock and tile and he blessed the water daily. After breakfast and catching up with his friends, Max took the shuttle into town, called Ubud Center, and sought out an herbalist recommended by his teachers from the ashram.

Kadek's Herbs and Ointments was the sign neatly painted on the front door. Max felt overwhelmed and was thankful the herbalist approached him when he made his way to the counter.

"Selamat siang. Welcome to Kadek's herb shop. I am Kadek." The diminutive Balinese man spoke with a big smile, bowing slightly with his palms together at the center of his chest.

"Selmat siang, Kadek, Max replied returning the bow with equal precision. I am Mr. Max from California and I would like to get your consultation on a selection of herbs. I am a friend of Ketut Arsana and I stay at Om Ham."

"Ahhhhh. Very good Mr Max. Tell me your needs and I will find you the perfect remedy. Let's go into the sitting room. My wife will prepare a cup of our home made tea and bring it so we can talk about what you want to find here."

"Terima Kasih, Kadek."

As the conversation evolved, Max learned that Kadek had herbs for every ailment, condition, or mental state a person wanted to either soothe or change. The Balinese people are very dedicated to their Hindu religion, and made daily offerings of fruit, food, money, incense and whatever they had at the time, to place at altars in their homes.

Religion is a main focus of their lives and if they had the time, would make as many as five offerings a day. They also had strong beliefs about both a dark and light side of the spiritual universe they lived in. Many Balinese families had roosters in cages and attended cock fights. When Max had asked Arta, his favorite yoga teacher, why he believed in cock fights, Arta very simply said, "Blood to earth, Max. Blood to earth." Max accepted that explanation and moved on. To this day, he has no idea what that really means.

Bali was so beautiful in so many ways and yet in others, it was hard for him to deal with. The famous Bali dogs are the perfect example. People get dogs and then don't have the money to feed them and the dogs end up wandering the mercilessly hot and humid streets getting in fights over food and water depending on the generosity of others to keep them alive. It was one of the harder things for him to learn to live with. He did his best, carrying a large bottle of water and bowl in his shopping bag so he could offer a drink whenever the opportunity presented itself.

He loved Arta and felt a special and unique connection to him from the first moment they met on a tour of the ashram two years earlier. As they walked through the ashram together going in and out of private rooms, and silent meditation caves if they were empty, Arta tapped his shoulder for them to stop. He then looked Max in the eyes and said, "I am here as your guide. Our mothers wish it to be."

Max didn't know why he was singled out and held back from the other guests who were on the ashram tour, but now he did. At first, he was typically upset that the rest of the tour was going to the healing room and he would miss it. Monkey mind at work. He knows better now, and was not there to change anyone but himself.

Max had his herbs in hand and his mind was racing in every direction. He purchased two very different bags. In one, the herbs he purchased would have the effect of making him very drowsy and put him in a slightly hallucinogenic state of mind. Too much at once could have a harmful effect on the nervous system and even be fatal. He was warned by the herbalist to stay at home, do yoga or meditate, and at the least just be still. If he did anything that required hand eye coordination, he could easily have an accident and get hurt. So climbing a mountain would be a life threatening exercise.

In the other hand, Max surprised himself and asked for a remedy or tonic, as he put it, to give him more energy for making love. It was the Balinese medicine man's version of Viagra. It had been three years since he was with a woman, but he already had feelings for Dori that were giving him hope he would use bag number two and flush away the other.

Love changed everything in Max's mind. He was a romantic. He wanted to have a "Best years of our lives" photo album featuring hundreds of photos of him and his lover on all the adventures that a couple could enjoy in a lifetime of being together. It just didn't happen. He had love in his life, but not the all encompassing love that kept people together for thirty and forty years. This gnawed at him in so many ways that sometimes he wanted to go to sleep and not wake up. Max had to laugh at himself as he was going over all this in his mind. He sounded like a Russian Poet. He stopped at a roadside coconut stand and ordered a drink.

He took another look at the little black bag of tea leaves and twigs that Kadek warned him about, and something that was only a thought in his mind now had the possibility of being very real if that was the path he was going to choose. Is this what he really wanted he started to ask himself? He actually knew it wasn't. Max was preparing for a day that deep down in his heart and mind, he knew he would not go through with. This was all drama for no good reason.

He started to get angry with himself. He just met a gorgeous woman and he liked her. Was it silly to think about starting over again and seeing if there was the possibility to have the only happiness that he really cared about anymore, the happiness that comes with being in love with a woman who would love him back? With that in mind, Max tossed the bag of herbs he knew he would never use in the huge trash bin sitting next to the coconut hulls.

He felt better already. Fuck the money situation. His Social Security check, while not enough to pay for a bad mobile home in a trailer park in Tornado Alley, here in Bali he could live like a king and be happy while doing it. He just arrived and he had enough money to live well for at least a few years, maybe even five or ten. Whatever. No more time spent on negative thoughts. Better to enjoy the hike, then the coffee and the food. He had so many of his favorite cafes and restaurants he wanted to eat at and places in Bali he had not seen yet. And who knows, he wondered. Maybe Dori would come to Om Ham and surprise him. He was still enjoying the romantic and erotic day dream he had about her and was somewhere in his mind thinking and hoping it could become real.

Max polished off his coconut and made his way over the broken, crowded sidewalks of Ubud to Sayuri Healing Foods. He came here as often as possible for both the food and the ambiance. It was one of those places that drew a unique yet not surprisingly, similar crowd almost daily. It also made him laugh in a heartfelt way, not in a mocking or condescending manner. He laughed, because he knew if he shouted out, "raise your hand if you are a Reiki Master," at least twenty hands would go up. He laughed again because half of the hands would be those of young men and women under the age of twenty five. Masters already. Everyone was on the same wavelength. Mindfulness ruled. As usual, it was packed, which was even better. He would always end up sitting with people he became happy to got to know. The scene inside reminded him of a somewhat similar setting at a very hip cafe in Los Angeles he would go to when feeling extravagant, Aroma Cafe. Aroma was located in Tujunga Village not far from the film studios and always had a crowd of industry types. A visit any day would find coffee mugs sitting on tables, laptops humming and plates of delicious looking food being eaten with gusto. It's a small world, the song goes. The nice thing for Max about being at Sayuri, was that most people had just come from a yoga class, not a Hollywood production meeting. The mood and energy was one of peace, calm, and community.

CHAPTER NINE

MOUNT BATUR

Max was ready for his mountain escape. He made arrangements with Udi, one of the drivers from Om Ham, to meet him at the reception desk at 2:00 A.M. This was the time that groups met to take the one hour drive to the mountain and then begin the slow hike to get to the top, five thousand six hundred and thirty three feet up from the starting point. That would get everyone at the vista point in time for a sunrise that was bound to be spectacular. There was not much preparation needed. Decent hiking shoes, a few layers of clothing to be worn as the temperatures changed on the way up, and a bag of snacks to keep your energy flowing has you covered.

He planned to stay in the area after the sunrise and just chill out enjoying the mountain. It was something new for him and being back at Om Ham could wait. He had no idea Dori was already on her way, but that was probably a good thing. It kept him present. Present was the only place to be when hiking up the steep and often wet crevices that led to the top. After three hours of careful steps and moments of never seen before views, he arrived.

He sat in full lotus from his perch at the top of Mount Batur as the sun began its ascent. The difficulty of the hike was long out of his mind. It was beautiful and inspirational. His mind slowed down as he practiced the meditation techniques he worked so hard to learn. There was only now. Breathe in, Breathe out. I am not this body, I am not even this mind.

Back down at the base of the mountain, Udi was there as promised and welcomed his friend into his car. He dropped Max at a beautiful group of bungalows called The Black Lava Hostel in Kintamani and waved goodbye wishing him a great day. Max was surprised in a good way when he saw the bungalows. He was not sure what to expect in such a remote area and for such a low price, but when he saw the hanging lanterns by each door and a beautiful garden just past the reception area, he knew he made a wise choice. The views were unmatched anywhere on the island and it was undeniably magical. Not very far under the moonlit sky, Mount Agung, which was nine thousand nine hundred and forty four feet up from sea level, was fully visible. It towered over everything else.

Most people think of the best beaches in the world when they think of a Bali vacation, but Bali is a four hundred square mile paradise of everything nature has to offer including four active volcanos and more than a dozen must see waterfalls.

Sitting in complete peace at one of the hostel's gardens, Max remembered a dear friend of his from Portugal, Joanna, who he met at Om Ham on his last visit. They did a day trip to the most arduous of all to reach, the dual waterfalls of Sekumpful and Fiji. They laughed and took videos driving in the van to get there and then making their way down the over five hundred steep wooden planks to get to the sand and water that led to the falls.

They stopped at a roadside restaurant on the way back to Om Ham to get some french fries. When he placed the order, the two young Balinese girls, no more than sixteen or seventeen, started laughing. He asked them, "what was so funny?" The girls giggled in that easy way girls do, and one of them said so innocently, "we think you look like Albert Einstein." Max laughed along with them. His hair was now long long, white, and unruly. And he was also happy that the girls from this far away land knew who Albert Einstein was.

So many memories. This time would be a solo experience, but remembering Joanna and the fun they had put an exclamation point on why Bali was so important to him and his well being. He was never alone unless he wanted to be. The guru would tell him his aura was glowing and that he was jealous that all the beautiful women want to be near him. The guru was teasing, of course, but Max knew he looked and felt better than any time in his life. Now he was at this beautiful mountain village alone to find that feeling once again while sitting in the beautiful and spiritual energy all around him.

The weight of the world seemed to have at least temporarily lifted off his shoulders. He walked through the small uneven streets of Kintamani with bright, clear eyes and feet that seemed to almost hover above the payment. Along his path, he made sure to stop in the local shops, looking at crystals and buying his favorite coffee and treats. He was happy to be free and walking in the small villages that were mostly untouched by the island's popularity. The roads were narrow and unpaved but the history and age of where he stood was palpable. As the sun began to set and the cooler mountain air prevailed, he turned to head back to his quiet bungalow for a good night's sleep.

As usual, life for Max was a bit dichotomous. He was so happy to be back at Om Ham and feel the love and support from all his friends there, and yet he felt like something happened to him on top of that mountain that wouldn't have happened if he didn't take this journey alone to be with himself and the powers of the universe.

The long flight from Los Angeles, meeting Dori, and reconnecting with all his friends had taken its toll in terms of energy spent. Not in a bad way, but as much as he liked to chat and meet new people, he was the kind of man who could enjoy twenty minutes of conversation and then be off on his way with a hug or handshake and a heartfelt "great to meet you." He wasn't a loner, but he was close.

Time in the mountains sleeping in the quiet comfort of the Black Lava Hostel did Max a world of good and were exactly what he had hoped for. He was relaxed with Bali life and a couple of days in the mountains were the perfect remedy.

Yoga, swimming, food, more yoga and meditation. Throw in the most delicious smoothie bowls on earth and becoming part of a crowd of happy smiling people and the recipe was complete. He wanted to stay longer, but he was lucky enough to score a cancellation for the time he was there. His room was due to be occupied the next day, so he had one more blissful night of spectacular sunsets and sunrises.

After a great breakfast of hot rice porridge with coconut milk and bananas, Max decided to take one final stroll through the small village and chat with the local shop owners. As he passed the registration desk, he heard the voice of a woman in distress. Something about money not available for two days and a credit card not working and where could she stay. He wanted to check it out and turned back to the desk and asked the woman whose back was still facing him if he could help in some way. The woman turned around and before she could say anything, Max held out his hand and introduced himself.

"Hi. I'm Max. I overheard a little of your conversation. Are you okay?"

Max was greeted with a teary eyed smile that did not detract even a tiny bit from the beautiful woman who just turned around to answer him. She was young looking, petite, with long curly blond hair and big blue eyes that at the moment were also a little red. She was wearing a man's flannel shirt, khaki cargo pants and tan Timberland hiking shoes on her feet.

I love Bali, Max said to himself for the millionth time. There is no other place in the world where so many people come face to face with someone they were destined to meet. Be it soul searching, life searching, or merely a happy travel adventure, the cosmic energy of Bali pulled and tugged on those who felt it.

"I can't get through to my bank and my credit card was eaten by the ATM yesterday in Ubud. I don't have enough money to pay for my room, the woman said, breaking Max's inner train of thoughts."

"That's horrible," Max replied. "The ATM's are notorious for that around here. Let me help you. How much do you need?"

"Really, the woman asked incredulously as she used her sleeve to wipe the redness out of her eyes?"

"Yes, Really. I'm happy to help. These kinds of things seem to happen a lot around here. What's your name?"

"Fleur."

"Nice to meet you, Fleur. That's a beautiful name. It fits you perfectly. Are you visiting from France?"

"Yes. I'm from Paris."

"I'm Max, from Chicago. Enchante'.

"Enchante', Max from Chicago. So, would thirty dollars be okay, she asked, getting right down to business. I can pay you back in two days."

"Done." Max reached into his pocket and pulled out a few hundred thousand dollar notes and handed them to Fleur. He had just enough with a little left over for lunch and a fun day in the village. "I'm walking into town, would you like to join me? It's my last day here and I want to explore a little."

"Oui oui, yes, s'il vous plait. Give me a minute to throw my backpack in my room and I will be right out. Thank you. Thank you very much." Fleur's outlook changed considerably. She was so excited to have a room and feel like things would be just fine, she spoke in French without thinking about it.

CHAPTER TEN

MAX, DORI, CHLOE

Back at Om Ham, Dori was getting out of the van while Wayan unloaded her two backpacks. The driveway was tucked between a small house with rooms for rent on one side and a scooter rental device on the other. Across the street was a small warung. A warung is local for diner. Westerners are told to be careful when eating at one without either seeing other Westerners eating there or hearing from someone who has eaten there and did not get sick.

For Californians, eating at a random warung would be like grabbing a quick piece of chicken off a food cart in Tijuana, Mexico without having Pepto Bismol in a coat pocket.

Dori loved the scene at the warung. Local people sitting at the counter, smoking their cigarettes, flirting with the waitresses, talking, joking. It wasn't that much different than a sidewalk cafe on Melrose Avenue in Hollywood she thought. Just a few hundred yards opposite the warung, when she walked under the tiled arches of Om Ham and past the massive statues of Ganesha and Hanoman she realized Melrose Avenue was actually quite far away.

"What do you think, Ms. Dori?" Wayan loved his life and culture in Bali and always hoped his guests would appreciate it and be interested in learning about it. His enthusiasm was contagious.

"It's beautiful, Wayan. Thank you so much." Dori paid Wayan for the ride and just stood near the reception desk taking in her surroundings. There were flowers and plants everywhere. A huge KOI pond filled with hungry fish puckering their mouths at the water's edge was next to the registration area. There were two Balinese style chairs with soft cushions and high backs beautifully carved with the faces of Shiva and other GODS the Balinese people celebrate.

There were tables containing short tour books about all the adventures available for the guests interested in day trips to the different islands or fun local trips to nearby waterfalls and mountains. And workers. She never saw so many people working so hard under a roasting hot sun. They were young and old, walking to rooms with trays of food, serving huge coconuts to sunbathers at the pool, and cleaning.

To Dori, it was a sight out of a Vietnam landscape where she could picture the short older men with the straw hats using those old style tightly wound whisk brooms. But it was right here in front of her and she loved it. She was happy to be here. For now, Thailand was far from her mind. She came to Bali on a lark, a spontaneous romantic quest. Surrounded by all this beauty she felt that no matter what happened she was good.

A beautiful young Balinese woman approached Dori with a registration form and led her to small sofa to fill it out. In the blink of an eye, another young staffer came over with a beautifully colored drink and a tray of cookies. The aroma of lemon grass plants growing like weeds was everywhere.

"Welcome to Om Ham, Ms Dori. My name is Koming. Your room will be ready for you soon. Please enjoy."

"Thank you, ummm Terima Kasih, Koming. What is this purple red drink?"

"Dragon fruit, Ms. Dori. Very delicious."

Koming smiled and walked back to the kitchen leaving Dori to sit, sip and let out a few deep breaths. No wonder Max loved this place so much she thought. It was beautiful beyond words and the people make you feel so welcome and important. Dori was not half way through her cookies and drink, when Eluh walked up with a big bowl of warm water and a tray of massage oils and salts.

Eluh was one of the massage therapists at the resort and was also a special assistant to the guru, learning about herbs and yoga from him each day and teaching basic yoga every afternoon on the grass opposite the pool and near the entrance to the pool and next to a huge Ganesh statue.

As Dori just took in each new sight and sound, workers and even some guests would walk by the statue and put an offering in the plate at the statue. Lord Ganesha is said to be the God of prosperity and wealth and his depictions were abundant on the island.

"Ms. Dori. I am Eluh. I give you welcome foot massage. Ok?"

"Yes. Very Okay, Eluh. Thank you. My feet are killing me."

Dori flipped off her sandals and let her feet drop gently into the warm salty water. Eluh poured a generous amount of the rough salt crystals into the palms of her hands and rubbed Dori's feet one at a time, lifting each one gently out of the water, scrubbing away old skin and placing each one back in the warm water to soak.

Next, Eluh poured a small amount of lavender oil into her palms and massaged the souls and calves of Dori's legs. Dori's eyes closed and she felt all her stress of travel and worry dissolve. The day didn't have to get any better than this she thought. Thank you, Max. Where are you, she was wondering? I'm here.

Dori loved her room. She had a long journey and took this unexpected detour, and all the while, she had no idea the man she came to find, was meeting someone new. She had just come back from her first Balinese massage and green tea scrub that was recommended by the therapist. It was heavenly and she was hungry and thirsty. She had no idea when Max would return, but she was perfectly content to enjoy the wonders of Bali she was just learning about.

The staff put her in a beautiful room on the second floor at the end of the tile hallway. Just outside her door was a beautiful view of the morning sunrise if she could force herself to wake up early enough. She was perfectly relaxed and it was the perfect time to call her friend Allie and give her the latest update. No romance to report on, but at least she followed through on what she knew was probably a very crazy idea. Time would tell.

Dori woke up feeling ready for her first full day at Om Ham. The breakfast in the Tulsi dining room was simple and delicious. She wasn't really a morning person, so a fresh coconut, dragon fruit smoothie and a side of scrambled eggs for some protein, was just right.

There was an 11:00 A.M shuttle into town so she had time for the 9:00 am yoga class and some shopping after. Dori made friends easily, so she was happy to see a lot of sandals at the entrance to the yoga room. Maybe she would meet someone who wanted to go into town. If not, she was a very happy solo traveler. First things first she reminded herself. Time for some Bali yoga. Max raved about kundalini tantra and she wanted to get at least one idea of what made him tick.

CHAPTER ELEVEN

MAX, FLEUR, KINTAMANI

It didn't take long for Max and Fleur to find out they shared a few things in common. They popped in and out of shops, trying on hats and sandals and the ever popular spiritual accessories like amulets and beads. These were the days Max lived for. No thoughts of anything other than the moment at hand. He was waiting outside a small bakery when he heard Fluer's voice calling for him. She had opened the front door a crack and in her sweet French accent asked him to come in. There was no resistance. Max already knew he would follow that voice anywhere.

Once inside the bakery, Max followed the sound of voices through a beaded curtain to a back room. Fluer was sitting at a table with an older woman dressed in ceremonial clothing. Balinese prints of Ganesh, Shiva and other Gods adorned the walls and a thick plume of incense floated a pacifying scent throughout the room. "Max, this is Ni Luh. She is the village palm reader and medicine woman. Can you imagine?"

The joy and excitement in Fluer's voice made Max smile. Here he was with a woman new to Bali leading him into the home of a village elder. May wonders never cease.

"I can imagine. Selamat paggi Ni Luh. I'm Max. Thank you for having us in your shop."

"You are welcome Mr. Max. Please sit next to Ms. Fluer. May I see your palm?"

"Do it Max. She already did mine. It was incredible."

Max hardly needed any encouragement for such experiences. One of his favorite places in Los Angele was a book store called The Third Eye, and every day there were at least five or six psychics or tarot card readers who were available for readings. Each person had their photo and a brief bio on the welcome board just outside the front door.

For Max, he went by the photo of the person. He was and always would be a visually driven person. It was always fun and if he got a reading that made sense to him, he liked it even more. Max held out his hand and Ni Luh took it gently to her forehead, then her heart, and back onto the table where she held his hand palm up with his fingers spread wide. She closed her eyes and chanted something in Balinese.

Fleur walked into the bakery section of the shop to give Max the same privacy she had. She was hungry and used her time to check out the menu. After looking over all the delicious choices, she bought a freshly made avocado, arugula and tomato sandwich for herself and another one for Max, along with some cookies for later.

Max came out of the small room with Ni Luh and bowed to her with his thank you and then gave a donation to her for both his and Fleur's reading. Ni Luh gave them each her blessing and they walked back out to the street feeling different than when they walked in. He was curious about the direction his life was taking and now he had Ni Luh's input to add to the equation.

"Thank you for this day, Max. For everything. Would you mind terribly if I walked back to the hostel myself? I'm ready to sleep and I have some things to think about."

"Of course not," Max replied. "This was a beautiful day. I really enjoyed being with you. Breakfast tomorrow morning before I head back to Ubud?"

"Yes. For sure. I ate while you were inside getting your palm reading and I bought an extra sandwich for you. Avocado, arugula and tomato. I split the cookies pretty evenly, she said with a grin as she handed the small bakery bag to him."

"That's very awesome. Thank you, Fleur."

"You're welcome. Wake me if I'm not up. Okay, she asked?"

"Okay," Max said.

Fleur gave him a very warm and intimate hug and a gentle kiss on his lips that lingered longer than a peck and then walked off leaving him with a warm feeling inside and hopes for a breakfast together in the morning. Max had no problem with Fleur wanting to go back to her room on her own, even though he could have sat with her for hours longer just listening to her soft, seductive French voice. Everything sounded better in French, even good-bye. Au revoir. Much better.

Max was back at his room just as the sun was setting, and too late for anything from the kitchen at the Black Lava Hostel. He was glad Fleur had the foresight to buy him a sandwich and some cookies at the bakery. As he ate, he thought about the palm reading Li Nuh gave him. She mentioned a woman he met recently and added that forever cliche, "nothing is as it seems". Anyone could say that about anything, he thought, but for a Twenty Thousand Indonesian Rupiah note, less than two dollars American, it was fun and Fleur really enjoyed her reading.

He was lying on his bed looking at the music choices on his tablet, when a knock on his door startled him. No reason to be paranoid he realized, so when he went to the door, and leaned in sideways to keep his naked lower half out of sight. Fleur was standing there in a pajama length t-shirt that hit her mid-thigh. The lettering fit her perfectly, spelling out "I'm too sexy for my shirt." Would anyone ever believe this, he wondered?

"May I come in? I don't want to be alone tonight."

"Sure, Max replied. Give me a second to get back under the covers then just come on in and close the door."

Fleur came in and sat on the edge of the bed next to him. He sat still, shirtless, his back against the headboard. The rest of him was neatly tucked under the sheets. "Are you okay," he asked?

"Yes. I just feel lonely. It's weird. I came up here to be alone, and now that I'm here, alone, I would love some company."

"Anything you want to talk about," he asked?

"Maybe later," okay? Fleur fumbled for the American way to say what she felt. "I have the busy mind, you know what I mean?"

"I can relate all too well. The guru calls it "Monkey Mind". I lost count how often I am the monkey he is talking about. Life is a trip, right?"

"Yes, oui". Fleur was smiling at their easy conversation. She was happy for this interruption from the thoughts that were making her sad and she felt free, open and uninhibited. Max loved these moments of complete surprise. Who wouldn't?

It felt extra good that she felt safe with him. He began to feel a lot more when Fleur smiled at him and pulled her pajama top over her head and tossed it to the floor with the casualness of a life long nudist.

Vive' la France, Max said to himself. He couldn't help but look, and she didn't mind. She peeled back the sheets and with a twinkle in her eyes, looked fondly at the rest of him. There was not a self conscious thought in her head as she slid her naked body under the sheets.

Max tensed a bit, then became still, frozen in the moment. "It's okay for me to share your bed? I should ask first?"

"Yes it's okay. Yes, usually ask first is good. At least for a man," he said laughing. He wasn't sure how much sleep he would actually get, but he would trade a sleepless night for Fleur's company in a New York minute. She stretched out next to him, resting her face on his chest. As she adjusted her body to find a comfortable position to sleep, she felt him aroused against her thigh. "ohhhhhh," she murmured.

"That's your fault," he conceded.

Fleur laughed and kissed him on the cheek. "We can sleep now," she asked with a most innocently teasing smile?

"Sure," Max replied. Give me a minute to settle in, and I'll be lights out in no time," he replied with only a slight hint of disappointment.

Fleur was not a tease and she did not feel obligated to do or say anything in particular. However, once Max was lying comfortably next to her and breathing calmly, she let her right hand slide down over him to that little crevice just below his tummy while her head rested softly on his chest. He was still aroused and doing his best to ignore it. Fleur, however, felt the exact opposite.

She was turned on as much as he was. She playfully wrapped her warm fingers around him for a moment, moving his aroused sex back and forth against his stomach in a slow tantalizing circle. She could feel him getting harder and then let go. She smiled as his cock just popped straight up, bobbing, staying hard against the sheet, waiting for her next move. Max let out a soft groan of pleasure.

She liked the way he felt in her hand. He was warm, and responsive to her every touch, growing more firm as she played. He tilted his neck forward looking at her hand, then her beautiful smile. "Better," she whispered not expecting an answer or waiting for one?

"It feels so good," Max replied softly.

Fleur's hand moved slowly under the sheet, her long blue fingernails snaking ever so slowly through his chest hair and then down over his cock. She pulled the sheet back out of sheer delight to admire her handy work and continue her sweet play.

She sat up in the bed and slid her butt closer to his so her hands could work together dancing all over him. His hips were thrusting involuntarily now, upwards and back, matching the rhythm of her hands. His groans became louder until he let out a deep, long sigh of relief. She smiled at him as he let go, emptying his, hot sticky mess. She was not a bit uneasy with the rawness of it all. She unwrapped her fingers from around him and smiled as Max's body relaxed and his breathing returned to normal.

Max looked up at her with glazed eyes. "Fleur.' Fleur got out of the bed. "Don't move, she ordered." She went into the bathroom, washed her face and hands, and came out with a warm washcloth for Max, which she then used to gently rub over his chest and legs.

"Wow, this is really full service," Max teased.

"What can I say? You're cute for an old guy. Now shhhhh."

She leaned in closer and gave him a sweet kiss. "Now we sleep," she whispered. She then rolled over on her side next to him to close her eyes and fall asleep. She felt warm and safe and was happy to feel his warm body against hers. Max was already sleeping, with slow peaceful breaths and a smile on his face. It had been a long time since he had sleepover company and it felt good.

CHAPTER TWELVE

OM HOME

Max was up early, enjoying a sunrise cup of coffee sitting at one of the breakfast tables to the side of the hostel. Sunrise in the mountains is always special with the unpredictable clouds and fog from the ocean breeze and the active volcano constantly changing the view. This day the sun was breaking through in levels between the clouds. It was one spectacular way to start the day. With the fresh memory of sleeping next to Fleur, the view came in second.

"Max, Fleur called out. Bon Jour."

Max turned around to see the beautiful smiling face of his new friend coming to sit with him.

"Bon Jour. You sleep okay?" Max asked. "Oui. C'e'tait magnifique. So peaceful here and such good company. What about you," she said with a twinkle in her eyes?

"Max smiled at her in a way he had not smiled at a woman in a long time. Then he tried to verbalize. "I was in such a deep sleep. I didn't even dream. You were my dream. That was so erotic and sexy. I didn't even know that was possible. They might have to bill me for the sheets."

"You're funny. May I go to Ubud with you? I have to be there to get my new credit card. I got an email from my mom last night and there is a bank on Monkey Forest Road that has it."

"Yep. The driver from Om Ham will be here in an hour. I'm going to hang out here."

"Okay. I'm going to get my things together and meet you in an hour. Ciao."

Sori, the head of the transportation and tour operations at Om Ham, was on time for a change. Of all the days Max called him for a ride, he managed to show up early the one day he wanted time to stop. Go figure.

The ride down the hill and through many small villages back to Om Ham gave Max and Fleur a few hours to get to know each other. They passed an early morning farmer's market, where they saw the village's residents sifting through the fruits and vegetables like any supermarket in their own home towns. One thing that was very different, however, was the sight of a man carrying a live chicken by the neck as he walked out of the market.

"You don't see that back home, do you, Max asked?"

"Not in the city, Max, but in the country, there are many small farms and French women are often found with an axe in their hands working hard. We are not afraid to cut off the head or skin the fish".

"Good to know, Max smiled. Remind me not to make you mad."

Sori cut in to give his perspective.

"Here, it is usually the man of the house. They go to market early in the morning while their wife or daughter is cleaning and making the offerings at the altar area outside their front door. Not everyone has big Western refrigerators and they get what they need each day. It's part of the day and it's all organic. That's why they are so small."

"I've noticed," Max replied. I ordered a chicken breast the other night for dinner, and I couldn't find it on my plate."

As Sori drove, Max enjoyed explaining a bit about the Bali culture and whatever he learned about the Hindu religion during his recent visits. Fleur revealed a little of her life as well and shared stories about her family, her travels, and her time at University.

All that was besides the point. The real reason she was in Bali was to try and make sense of her father's recent death. He was her best friend and she idolized him. She was only twenty years younger than her dad, and they grew up close. There were no secrets and by the time she was five, she had already installed him as the hero in her life. His death was sudden and took her by such surprise she felt lost. She knew her mom was also devastated, but there was nothing she could do. She flew to Bali with her mom's blessing to stay and heal and find her spirit. Her father would have expected no less.

As much as Max enjoyed being with Fleur, he also felt free to share that he met someone on the flight to Hong Kong and that it felt like there was a real connection and one he felt was worth exploring. He told Fleur that he invited her to Om Ham for a few days but wasn't sure if she would come. They didn't share email or phone numbers so most likely it would just be one of those passing ships in the night. Or in this case, a great way to spend five hours between flights. But he did hope she would come find him.

Fleur was genuinely supportive and happy for him. Then he shared details of his recent break up, which for him, was only slightly less devastating to him than Fleur's reasons for coming. He talked about the loss of his mom, and she talked about the loss of her dad. Together they both could say that no matter a person's age, when our moms or dads pass on, there is a void that no amount of time can really heal. We learn to accept that parental bonds are always with us and even seem to grow more powerful as time passes, not something we forget.

By the time Sori's van pulled into the Om Ham parking lot, Max and Fleur found a closeness and a friendship neither had expected. Their conversation was real and honest about things in life that affect us on deep and personal levels. He was happy to be that older voice of reason, and she seemed happy to have someone to confide in who was not hitting on her. She even admitted she was mostly into girls but didn't like to box herself into corners when it comes to dating.

Fleur enjoyed being with men from time to time and she valued the closeness and intimacy with women she felt an attraction to. If there was a spark, so be it. Max appreciated that. Love everyone, one his favorite mentors, Ram Das, always said.

He helped her out in a way many people helped him more than once and it felt good to return the kindness.

With that in mind, he booked a separate room for Fleur when they passed the registration desk. He knew she still didn't have her credit card and he didn't see any need to wait for her to ask or feel like she was supposed to stay with him. They agreed to meet at the pool later if possible and if not, well, C'est la vie as they say. Little did Max know, Dori had arrived a couple days earlier and was in a room just above his.

The pool at Om Ham was a healing experience and Max would make sure to get in and at least splash around once or twice a day. He liked to swim until his arms got tired and then walk the length of the pool until his legs got tired. All in all, a full body workout he would say. The water was warmed by the everyday sunshine and the energy was enhanced by the statues of Hindu Gods and the daily blessings from the guru, Ketut Arsana.

Fleur had made it to the pool first, and was kind enough to lay out a towel for him on the chaise lounge next to hers. Max thought about how great she looked in her flannel shirt and boots walking around town the previous day, but she looked like a runway model in the string bikini she had on at the pool. He called ahead to the Tulsi dining room across from the pool, and just as he sat down next to her, Koming walked up with two big coconuts on a tray with spoons for the meat and bamboo straws for the juice.

"Thank you, Max. And thank you for the room. I will pay you back tomorrow."

"You're welcome, Fleur. I'm happy to help. How's your room?"

"It's perfect. I'm just upstairs from you in 208. I checked out the yoga room. Wow. It's really so beautiful and the views of the rice fields are incredible. I can understand why you like it here so much."

"It's the perfect place to deal with what you are going through. It's perfect for anything, really. If it's okay with you, I would like to introduce you to my friend and teacher. He teaches the master yoga class Sunday morning and he is also an amazing healer."

"I would love to, Fleur beamed. I guess losing my credit card turned out to be a good thing."

"I'll drink to that," Max replied while raising his coconut up to his lips for a sip of the sweet juice. Fleur raised hers and did the same. "You're funny and sweet, Max. It's nice to be with you. He could only smile and shake his head. There were no words.

He could only think that once again, the magic of Bali brings light into any dark space. He and Fleur spent time in the pool doing laps, drinking their coconut juice and talking about life. Their time together was effortless and Max loved how open and honest they were with each other. He learned she is only twenty eight and as big a difference as that was between them, it didn't seem to matter one bit.

They connected on a more spiritual level. It was a deeper level than swiping right or left for a date. And as much as Max maintains age is only a number, forty years is a lot of life lived. Bottom line, it wasn't important for now and it wasn't important here. Even his male friends were younger.

It was just who he was as a person. He had a young heart and an old soul. When it came to discussing age, Max liked the way one of his very first yoga teachers explained it. Yogi Bhajan always said a person is only as old as his spine. What about the knees Max wanted to know?

After some sun and a few laps, Max left Fleur at the pool to enjoy her swim and her shuttle into town. She was sweet and affectionate to him, but he also knew that what happened the night before, was most likely a one time experience.

Whatever it was, he would just be himself and let things happen as they will. It was the perfect time for a midday nap. He knew as soon as he put on some Krishna Das music he would be lights out. He didn't want to sleep through dinner, but he also liked going to bed hungry. He found it led to more vivid dreams and he loved waking up looking forward to breakfast. It was win win.

CHAPTER THIRTEEN

DORIS DOES YOGA

As Dori explored the yoga room getting ready for her first class, she at once understood why Max was so impressed with the environment here. The set up was truly different from any class she ever went to in Los Angeles. The hotel staff had laid out all the yoga mats on the polished hardwood floor and there was a beautiful altar area that was slightly raised from the floor and covered with a white sheepskin throw. It was at the front of the room in the center facing out towards the students.

Much to her delight, there was also a woman about her age, placing Tibetan singing bowls in a circle just in front of the Guru's altar or whomever was teaching that morning. Max had raved about his favorite teacher, Arta, and she was hoping it would be him for her first class.

Dori's eyes lit up when she saw the teacher walk in, followed by a few more students. He was tall, with long dark hair and dark eyes that could look into your soul. He unpacked his harmonium and did a few stretches on his white sheepskin throw rug and then introduced himself.

"Hello friends. I am Arta. We are doing kundalini tantra this morning. Is anyone here for the first time?"

His voice was deep and resonating and powerful. He was confident in every word and action he took. Dori's hand went up as did a few others scattered around the room. She felt good not to be the only first timer, but had settled onto a yoga mat in the middle of the room for the sake of blending in.

It was just like that feeling in a high school or university class when you were not sure of yourself and would grab a seat in the back hoping not to be noticed. Of course, that never worked. But here and now, it was yoga and the space was there for all to enjoy equally, first time or tenth. Arta played a few chords and then looked out at his students and just simply said "Ready."

Immediately everyone sat in lotus pose with backs straight and he started chanting AUM. There were the usual three AUM chants and then here, it was followed by Om Shanti Om. That was new for Dori, but she fell into the rhythm of the class and regardless of what else the day might bring, she knew this was a great start. By the time class had ended, she could feel the spiritual difference Max told her about and how it related to more intense chanting in the Bali style yoga.

She was calm in her mind, yet her body felt the effects of a solid ninety minute workout. Once class was over and everyone was lying on their backs, palms up in shivasana, or corpse pose, Arta's assistant played her singing bowls while eyes closed and tensions evaporated.

The grand finale took Dori by surprise and was the best part of all. She heard Arta walking around the room, and opened her eyes to see what was going on. He moved from student to student, resting his palms on their heads for a moment, letting his healing energy sink in, and then moving on to the next person.

She quickly closed her eyes to get back into the moment. She heard an occasional groan or loud Ahhh or Ohhh, and she thought it must be very nice. The next thing she knew, Arta had her head lifted a few inches above her mat and in the blink of an eye, he gave a twist and the whole class heard a series of cracks. It was one vertebra after another getting the tension snapped out. Then she let out a long, loud Ohhhhhhh…. She had no control of it. It felt so good, it just came out.

"Feel better, Arta asked?"

Dori could barely speak. She had not had a release like that since any time she could remember. All she could really think about was that her mind felt at a different level of consciousness. Her body felt limp.

"Thank you, she said in a whisper."

That neck twist or adjustment as some might call it, was all she could think about as the shuttle bus made its way into town. She was happy with her choices and proud of herself for taking the chance to take this spontaneous side trip. She had a great massage and a great yoga class and now she felt so good she wanted to buy everyone she knew a gift. She knew she was feeling free and easy when she realized how much she was spending and how much she was eating. She couldn't help but compare Ubud, Bali to Los Angeles California, and wondered to herself if she, like Max, could live here. The differences, of course, were stark.

In LA, a person could not walk a block or two without passing a pot dispensary. Here, in Ubud, it seemed a person could not walk a block or two without passing some kind of amazing food, yoga shop, or ice cream stand. Gelato was popular and on every corner, and cheap. The more she walked, the more often she would pass a store Max told her about. Right there in front of her, she saw the Wooden Spoon.

Max raved about this place with all the breads and sweets and teas, so this was a must. She spent way too much time at the counter picking out treats. Chocolate almond croissants and fruit tarts stood out and in no time at all, she had a take out bag full of goodies. She needed a break, so when a table opened up she sat down with her first charcoal tea latte and pumpkin spice scone. Unbelievable was all she could think to say as she ate and drank and felt all the joys of exploring someplace new.

Her phone rang, and when she saw the California digits her eyes lit up. For a moment, it felt like being home and getting a phone call. "Allie. How are you, you little slut?"

"Me? Ha. You're the one eight thousand miles away chasing after a man with long white hair and prayer beads." They both were laughing out loud. The customers at the table behind her all looked up for just a moment, but then went back to their food. No judgments or harsh words. No, "Hey lady, can you keep it down."

Life is good, Dori thought as she listened and talked and enjoyed her snack. She gave Allie the most recent Max update, which was nothing, so they caught up on Allie's life and even a little business. Allie was an important friend in her life, and she couldn't have taken the time away from work without her. She would surprise her with something nice on her next shopping trip.

Before she could even get to the shuttle area, she was lured into a very beautiful massage room. It's hard to walk a block in Ubud without hearing the words, "Massage Mister, Massage Miss". It was only $3.50 for a thirty minute foot massage, and it was impossible to say no. Who would want to? Sometimes when it is hotter than usual and you don't want to get undressed, it's just perfect to lie back in a lounge chair and let the Balinese women work their magic. When her turn came, she fell back onto her chair and closed her eyes.

By the time she made it back to her room, she was glad she took a few moments earlier to put things away and hang a few outfits in the closet. She had nothing else to do but enjoy a long, long hot shower and take a rest. She decided she would put Max out of her mind for a while and just enjoy her surroundings.

The shower was great and resting on her bed in the full length cotton robe provided by the hotel had her thinking of the great spa days she would share with Allie back in Los Angeles. It was ultra plush and felt great against her still tingling and revitalized skin. She had that contented smile of being in a state of bliss. She was fortunate to have the financial security back home to enjoy a massage whenever she wanted one, and she fully believed in pampering oneself for no special reason other than it felt good.

It was not quite sundown, and she could barely keep her eyes open. The time on the clock didn't matter. For Dori, the days and nights were so jumbled together, she decided sleep would be her best choice. There would be no Max updates for now. She would knock on his door in the morning or find him in the breakfast room he told her about.

CHAPTER FOURTEEN

MAX AND FLEUR

Max was sleeping when Fleur tapped softly on his door. She knew he was there, so she walked in quietly and sat on the edge of his bed next to him. She gave him a gentle shake, rubbing his back in a soothing way from his tailbone to his neck and shoulders. He moved a tiny bit, but didn't wake up.

With her fingers kneading the knots in his neck and shoulders, he finally turned his head around slowly. He saw his sweet friend looking cute as ever. She was in a long sleeve button down peach colored shirt that was completely open. It clung loosely to her breasts and went down far enough past her waist to cover the area where panties would have been.

"I'm glad it's you," he said laughing in his sleepy voice. That feels nice." Max noticed the redness in her eyes as much as he noticed her beauty. "What's wrong? Come sit next to me."

Fleur took off her shirt and got under the covers next to him. She kissed him on the lips and let one hand rest on his chest, twirling her fingers between his chest hairs. "You are a sweet man, Max. I'm fine. I just don't want to be alone."

It didn't take long for him to react to her touch. His sex began to push up the thin white sheet he was sleeping under and her eyes went straight to the tent he was creating. She was wet with her own excitement and was happy to see his instant reaction.

"I would like to stay with you tonight. It feels good for me. I think it is okay for you, yes," she said with a sexy smile looking at his erection.

"Is that a trick question," Max asked?

Fleur didn't answer with words. She flashed her playful smile and slowly brushed her hands over the bedsheet, stopping for just a second over the bulge just below his waist. She lingered there, looking into his eyes and let her long mane of shiny blonde hair dance over his face and chest moving down slowly, seductively, until her lips covered him where her hands were. She teased him over the sheet, biting, licking, and kissing in combination with her hands sliding up and down the length of his shaft.

The friction was unbearable, and Max's waist lifted up a bit from the bed, his excitement taking over. His hips moved on their own upward to meet Fleur's teasing mouth. The combination of the silky thin material of the sheets in between her warm hands and moist lips was more than he could take. She loved feeling him grow in her hands, and began to move around sliding next to him while allowing her fingers to do a little more teasing. With the eagerness of a child holding a new toy, she pulled the sheets back, tossing them aside to lie naked next to him.

She began slow strokes up and back, base to tip, with her fingernails leading the way; a little twist, a French twist if you will, before resting her hands on his belly. Max was as excited as he had ever been, the evidence just below her treacherous hands, pulsing with a heartbeat of its own. She couldn't resist giving him a little attention in the form of a gentle slap back and forth. His manhood stood at attention, moving a little on its own, hungry for her next move.

Fleur was merely being her playful self. Her sexy self that was indulging in an escape she so desperately needed. She was turned on by how much he was turned on and she enjoyed being in charge of this sweet, naughty episode. She was miles from home and free of all the thoughts that burdened her. She loved holding this man's cock in her hands and owning it. Tonight, it was hers.

"Turn over and close your eyes," she commanded.

Max did as told, even though it was a bit uncomfortable to lie on his stomach in the condition he was in. But Fleur already knew that. She was playing the role of a young Fem Dom with Max as her submissive. She poured some oil in her hands, and let her legs drape over his body resting her hips on his lower back. The heat between them only fueled their desires. She applied what must have been the perfect amount of pressure as her long strokes up and down his back started to emit groans of pleasure. Her fingers were long and skilled, alternating light and strong touch, working muscles and knots as well any little crevices she could find. Her fingers found that tender spot between his butt and penis, and he nearly lifted off the table when she probed between his cheeks, ever so delicately with her index finger. She was a curious little cat.

Max groaned softly and he began to move his hips. Sensing he was close to orgasm, Fleur slid her fingers under him and gently turned him over onto his back. Finally, Max was thinking. He didn't know how much more he could take. She could feel the moisture between her legs and her own release building. It felt good. She used one hand to guide him inside her slowly until he reached where she wanted him to go.

He froze for just a moment, in pleasure and that unique sensation of being in a woman's sacred place. She moved with the presence of an old soul experienced in the art of love. She slid down further, filling herself with him, arching forward to let her breasts and pert brown nipples reach his mouth. Slowly, deliberately, she moved from side to side.

She would rest long enough for each one to get the attention she craved. She was an expert tease delighting in her own power and the lustiness Max showed in taking her breasts between his teeth, sucking, nibbling, devouring. He delighted in tasting her and being on the receiving end of her passion.

She was an open lover and did not shy away from looking into his eyes with her hands on his shoulders. She moved so slowly, almost still, right up to that moment she felt him quiver and gush inside her. His body spasmed involuntarily, totally spent. She then eased off of him allowing their bodily fluids to merge and slid forward on his oiled body until she was resting her wet pussy on his face. She rotated slowly on his parted lips, rocking gently until she felt herself letting go of her own pent up tension and stress.

Max was deliriously unconscious in his movements, letting Fleur be his guide. He barely noticed the beautiful tattoo of a small Monarch butterfly over her heart. She used her body motion to take care of herself and Max at almost the same time. That part wasn't planned. It just happened all on its own and she knew she gave her partner all of her at a time they both needed to share something so powerful and healing for body, mind and heart. Fleur had a smile on her face. She let go of everything inside her, cumming intensely. Max didn't flinch and helped her let go, rejoicing with her and savoring all of her. They sank to the bed, doused in sex and at ease with the pleasure they gave each other. They shared a cosmic delight and touched each other's soul, and the DNA they shared would make them part of each other forever.

Fleur had a deep sleep and remembered the lust and love she just experienced as her eyes opened slowly in the middle of the night to see her legs still slightly tangled to the legs of her lover. She got up quietly and gave Max a sweet kiss on the lips. "Good night, Mr. Max." She slid out of the bed, grabbed her shirt and put it on as she walked up the stairs to her room.

CHAPTER FIFTEEN

MAX, DORI AND FLEUR

Morning came too quickly, as it always does when you never want the night to end. Max's eyes opened slowly. The longer this could last the better, he thought. He was still on his bed, naked with remnants of oil and Fleur filling his senses of sweet memories and pheromones of love and sex. He moved his hands left and right hoping to make body contact with any part of her. No such luck.

He was doing his best to wake up and was happy to feel sore where he had not been sore in a long time. He didn't even remember falling asleep and he had no idea of when Fleur left. He noticed the bunched up sheets and the memory of her hands and body parts all over him came flooding back like he was looking through one of those virtual reality headsets.

He would keep room service out today. He wanted these sheets all to himself for another twenty four hours. His mind flashed to Dori briefly, still not knowing she was right there upstairs. As much as he wanted to see her again, he could barely think of anyone else right now. The sun was coming up and the familiar sound of the roosters crowing was all he needed to come awake and savor the aroma all around him. As he came out of his trance, he saw the note on the nightstand. "See you tomorrow, Max. I didn't want to wake you. Fleur."

Max put on his yoga mantras and went about his daily ritual of making his morning coffee. He could do this in his sleep, so being able to relive the pleasure of the hours earlier were his companions. That, and a strong cup of single origin Sumatra dark roast coffee with a splash of oat milk. He would let the rest of the day unfold as it came.

Upstairs, Fluer was sitting at the little bistro table outside her room. She was enjoying a hot cup of lemongrass tea and the last peanut butter cookie she got from the bakery in Kintamani. It reminded her of the fun day she had with Max and the reading she got from Li Nuh, the village palm reader. Li Nuh told her to let her emotions come out, that her father was with her, watching over her, and wanting her to be happy for all the love they shared.

She said specifically her father wanted her to stick with her studies and to live the life she truly wanted, not a life anyone else expected of her. Fleur told Li Nuh about Max, and how he loaned her money for her room and she asked if it was okay for her to be with him at such a crazy time in her life. Li Nuh nodded positively at the mention of Max's name and assured Fleur she was safe and with someone who is protective in nature and would look out for her.

One last thing that sent goosebumps up her arms, was when Li Nuh said her father was right in the room behind her, and said to be brave, and to be strong for her mother. That brought tears and the sense of calm Fleur came to Bali to find. While she sat there watching the sun come up remembering those words and listening to the roosters, she heard the door open from the room next to hers.

Dori was still sleepy in a pleasant kind of way. Nowhere to rush to, nothing to do but enjoy the stillness of early morning and this gorgeous view of the rice fields from her window. When she stepped outside, she noticed a family of ducks taking a slow paddle in the trenches of water that surrounded the rice fields just a few hundred yards past the pool. Mamma duck and all her babies single file as if they were in a parade. It *was* a parade of sorts, as within minutes, the roosters obliged with their version of a morning roll call. A peaceful start to the day and perfect for staying in her lingerie style pajamas of soft hemp and lace. They fit her like they were made for her, showing off her legs and breasts to the warmth of the sun as it started its slow rise from the East.

"Hi. I didn't know I had a neighbor, Dori said when she saw the cute young woman sitting at a table next to her door. I didn't hear you come in. My name is Dori."

Fleur was still in her gray drawstring shorts from the night before. She wasn't in them that long anyway. She was sitting with her knees up, feet on her chair. Her legs were long, beautiful and tan. Her top was a white button down Tommy Bahama beach shirt, unbuttoned, of course. It hung perfectly on her body, moving as she moved. Who needs buttons?

"Hi, I'm Fleur. I'm glad I was quiet. It was very late. My father always told me I walk like Sasquatch. Here comes Bigfoot, he would say."

"Ha. That's cute. Very Daddy's girl. Was that you, Dori asked?"

"Yes. He was a young dad so we went almost everywhere together. He and my mom were both young and silly and I got to share in a lot of craziness. What about you? Were you close with your father growing up?"

"I was a different kind of Daddy's girl. More the business daughter. I started going to his office with him in my junior year of high school. He loved me like a son, his friends would say. But he would have always done anything in the world to help me if I asked. So,… Fleur is a French name? Flower if my college French is working at this early hour?"

"Yes, oui, Paris. Parlez vous Français?"

"A little, but I always want to learn more, Dori replied with a smile. So, where did you come from tiptoeing your way back to your room in the middle of the night, if I may ask? You have a very happy grin on your face. Is there romance blooming in the rice paddies?"

"Ha. No, no. I was downstairs visiting with a friend. We both fell asleep. I woke up first and you know, sometimes with a man it's nice to just escape and talk later. They ask so many questions after, n'est pas?"

"Yes, oui. N'est pas indeed, Dori replied. You're a funny girl. I didn't hear a thing. Your father would be proud. Maybe he can give you a new nickname."

Fleur's head looked down for just a moment. "My father passed away last month."

"Oh my God," Dori said feeling embarrassed. "I'm so sorry. Please forgive me."

"It's okay," Fleur replied. How would you know?

The girls meshed well together and their conversation flowed in both French and English.

"So, tell me about your friend. You must like him to spend the night with him. Did you come here together?" Dori asked.

"We did come *here* together, but not to Bali. I came by myself to be alone and think about my dad. It's weird. I like to be alone to figure things out, but it feels better being able to talk with nice people."

"I get it," Dori replied. "There are no easy answers. Do what feels right. This is a safe place to explore your emotions and learn to trust yourself."

"Did you come alone, Fleur asked?"

"I did. But, of all things, I met this man on the plane and he told me if I had any extra time, I should come visit him at Om Ham and explore the island and do some yoga. We seemed to have a really great connection, So… I decided to take a chance. Is that silly?"

"No. It's sweet. It's totally romantic," Fleur offered with an encouraging smile. In a more mischievous tone, she asked," is he in your room?"

"Ha! That's cute. I wish, but he's not even here to take a shot at it. He left a message with the staff to take good care of me, and that he was up in the Kintamani mountains at a small hostel doing some hiking for a couple of days. Bad timing for me, I guess. Maybe I should move on and explore something else."

Fleur's brain was slowly waking up and as she listened to Dori's answer, she had the weirdest thought. Max had mentioned a woman named Dori and that he invited her to Bali. There could not be more than one Max and Dori, right, she asked herself?

She hoped they could change the topic. Her sleepy suspicions were being confirmed before she could rub her eyes and make them go away. This is her. Now what, she thought to herself?

"Will you stay and wait a few days," Fleur pleaded trying to delay the inevitable? It is really nice here and Max told me the yoga was amazing."

"MAX? Did you just say Max told you the yoga was great?

"Baiser,"(fuck) Fleur muttered in disbelief.

"I know that word," Dori said. Her words were soft spoken but her tone told a different story. "What's going on? You look like the girl with her hand in the cookie jar. Does this Max have long white hair, beads and crystals. Is he funny and cute?"

"Yes, and yes. I have to tell you something. That's where I was. I met him at the hostel."

"And last night? Those were your cute little sandals on his welcome mat?"

Fleur rattled on. "Yes, but you have to understand. I lost my credit card and couldn't pay for my room. He heard me crying at the registration desk. I was a mess and he helped me out."

"Okay. Please go on, if there's more."

"A little more," Fleur added. We walked around town and hung out. Then he brought me here yesterday so I could get to the bank and get my new credit card. That's pretty much everything."

"And last night? Are you staying with him now," Dori Asked?

Fleur was quiet, feeling stuck in the middle of something she had no idea of or wanted any part of. She certainly didn't need any love triangle drama. "Well, Dori asked impatiently as her smile faded?"

"I'm not staying with him. I'm *your* neighbor. He got me this room to be by myself. He's not like that. He's a good guy. It was all me. I was feeling lonely and I really needed the company."

Dori was quiet, gathering her thoughts. This was the last thing she would have expected here in Bali of all places. Los Angeles, sure. But here?

Fleur continued, just wanting to get it all out and be done with it. "How could I know the woman he told me about was you, and that you would be here? Right? And neither did he. He told me he hoped you would come but he had no way to contact you. He talked about you a lot, even after we… Seriously, we are only friends. I'm sorry for this to be so…"

"Baiser," Dori said, saying the words for her. I'm sure you are, she added a bit sarcastically."

"I'm sorry, Dori, it's the same man as you. Are you unhappy with me?" Fleur looked genuinely sad and beautiful at the same time. Much to Dori's dismay, Fleur's pouty lips only made her look cuter.

"Well, I don't exactly want to take you out for a night on the town," Dori threw back. She looked at her sexy, young neighbor in hardly any clothes who had the modesty of a porn star, then added, - "At least not right now."

"I would go to dinner and dance with you, Fluer said. I actually prefer girls more if that helps." The two women just looked at each other and all of a sudden Fleur laughed.

"It's dining and dancing, you little tart." Dori knew she was not really mad, but she couldn't resist one more poke if she could get away with it. "I should just go back to Thailand and do my own thing as I intended in the first place."

"No. Stay here, Fleur insisted. All the way here in the van he was saying he hoped you would show up."

"Well, that's a nice thought. I wonder if he is still hoping."

"He is. I know it. Don't be mad with me. I want to be friends. It was just sex. He was mostly sleeping, anyway. I was just in a mood. I went into his room to hang out a little and have company. I got in the bed and it just happened. You know?"

"Yes, Dori replied. I know. That does happen when you get into bed with a man. More often than not. N'est pas?"

"You're still mad. You know, in France, many women will have the same lover. It's acceptable in our culture. Sometimes even mother and daughter will share the same man, but that can be dangerous for the man. You know what I mean?"

"You're a funny girl, Ms. Fleur. I'll have to look into moving to Paris."

"Ha! You're joking. So everything is okay? You will stay here and be my neighbor?"

"Can you keep your sexy little ass to yourself for a day or two so I can say hello to this guy?"

Fleur felt relieved. "So you think I have a sexy ass? You won't be mad at Max?"

"Yes to the ass, no to being angry with Max. But I may have to make him suffer a little first, eh?"

"You're evil, Fleur said grinning. You and Max will be a good couple. So no more talk about that. There is a two hour master yoga class today with the guru of the ashram and it starts at 9:00. Go with me?"

"I wouldn't miss it," Dori replied. Her anger subsided and her smile returned. Fleur was like a little magnet for fun. If she were Max she had no doubt she would have also enjoyed this sweet woman's charms. As for enjoying Max's charms, she would have to think about that.

CHAPTER SIXTEEN

YOGA DAY FOR ALL

Max had some time before yoga class and he was still processing the great night he had with Fleur. He still couldn't believe it. All alone at the top of a mountain, an angel drops into his life like she was put on earth just for him. He was too happy to stand still, so he grabbed his backpack filled with treats for the staff, and stepped onto the neatly cut bricks that took him to the registration office and the entrance to the Tulsi Dining Room.

His smile was broad, and if one could see auras there was a golden yellow aura dancing around his head from ear to ear that would only moderately describe his state of euphoria coming down from the mountain. Of course, he was not yet aware that his new friend Fleur was upstairs talking to his other new friend, Dori.

"Mr Max, Govinda shouted out. Where you go?"

Max laughed remembering that when he first arrived in Bali and someone would approach him like that, he would be uneasy. Back home if a stranger asked him "where you go" he would either keep walking or stop long enough to say, "None of your business."

In Bali, Max learned it was merely the pure interest of the staff at his hotel wanting to know what he was planning to do that day or what he had done earlier. No ill intentions, nothing to fear. It's a different world when a person no longer needs to be suspicious of everyone they don't know.

"Good morning Govinda, Max said while politely bowing forward with his palms together at his heart center. I did the early morning hike up to Mount Batur and spent some time in Kintamani. In fact, I have a little surprise for you all."

Max unhooked from his backpack and let it fall to the ground. He reached inside and pulled out a big bag of assorted pastries and sweets. In America, cookies are a normal occasion and joy to indulge in. In Bali, $.75 cents for a cookie is a luxury these workers could not afford and bringing these gifts made him feel happy inside.

"What is it, Mr Max?" Govinda was like a kid waiting to see what his father or uncle brought home from a vacation out of town. At least, with Max. He was wearing the yellow Nike rain jacket Max gave him on his last trip and the two enjoyed a special bond. The manager at Om Ham told him privately that Govinda wore it every day.

Max opened the bag and pulled out a big tray of homemade "power balls". These were popular all over the island and made with cashews, raisins and non dairy milk with a sprinkling of chocolate on top. He held the tray out for Govinda and Sori, who were lucky enough to be present at the right time.

"Take a few and a few for the restaurant staff," Max suggested. "I brought these down from Kintamani."

"You look very happy, Mr Max," Sori chimed in with his usual big smile. His English was excellent.

Sori had taken Max on a few trips and was known as a bit of a playboy. He drove mostly the guests at Om Ham's sister resort called Ubud Aura, located inside the community at the Yoga Barn. It was primarily a yogi and yogini mating site for the spiritually obsessed.

Any Hollywood producer worth his salt would make a weekly series out of it and it would be a hit show if he or she was any good. It was a job Max would have loved when he was Sori's age. It sure beat the hell out of driving for Uber in Los Angeles.

"I feel amazing. The sunrise was amazing. Everything is amazing, Max laughed." Max was giddy and smiling the smile he had most days he was in Bali. He was home. This time, he did not plan to leave.

"Mr Max. Your friend Fleur asked me for a ride to Ubud Aura to check out the Yoga Barn. She's very pretty. Do you like her?"

"She's just a friend. And you be nice to her. None of your playboy stuff. Got me?" Max was smiling as he said it, but he was only half way joking.

"No problem, Mr. Max. You know, it's you who is the playboy."

"What are you talking about, Sori?"

"There is another beautiful woman here to see you. Ms Dori. We put her in room 206."

Oh my God was all Max could think of, and he said that to himself. He could only wonder what to do next. He was hoping Dori would come but he had no idea he would have female company when she arrived.

"Thank you. I appreciate that. We met at the airport in Hong Kong. I had no idea she would come. So she is in room 206," Max asked hoping he heard wrong.

"Yes, Mr. Max. She is right next to your other girlfriend in 208. The guru and all the staff are talking about it. You will need Guru's special tea for energy." Sori was always happy to tease Max about his age when the subject was women.

Govinda jumped in to get Max's attention. "Mr Max, is room 118 good for you?"

"Yes, Govinda. Thank you so much. I love that room. It's perfect. Thank you so much. I think this calls for a pizza. What do you think?"

"Yes, Mr Max. Thank you."

Govinda just bowed silently. Max returned the bow and retreated to his room to get ready for yoga class while wondering what kind of greeting he would get when he saw Fleur and Dori. He had no intention of doing anything to hurt Dori and yet he felt like he did.

The only saving grace was that this was completely unintentional. Max had no way of knowing Dori was here. They never exchanged numbers or even e-mail. But that would not make her feel any better. She flew to Bali instead of Thailand just to spend time with him. He had an hour before yoga to figure something out.

He left the reception desk feeling that all too familiar knot in his stomach he worked so hard to keep at bay. He did not like confrontation, and he didn't like avoiding issues that must be faced sooner or later. He preferred sooner. So he walked slowly, thinking that maybe a yoga mat at the back of the room and close to the exit door could work as a happy medium. One thing for sure, he would find out soon enough.

The class was mostly full, and after a quick scan of the room, Max spotted Fleur and Dori, sitting side by side on their mats, facing the guru. They seemed as comfortable as two old friends at a college reunion. And as if he settled onto his mat like a kitten wearing a bell around his neck, their eyes turned towards him simultaneously as he eased into full lotus position.

Fleur smiled and waved, motioning him to come over. Dori just smiled and mouthed a silent hello. Max chose to stay where he was with the hope that the guru's master set of yoga poses, meditation, and intense breathing would get everyone into a loving, peaceful, maybe even forgetful, frame of mind.

Leaning on the rail just outside the yoga room and facing the rice fields and pool, Govinda and Sori were whispering and smiling. Max assumed they were amused about the position he would find himself in once class was over. They were both kind and loving souls, but that had nothing to do with them discussing and enjoying the potential fate of a man who would soon find himself confronted with two women he was interested in; One he already slept with, and one he hoped to. Where was that famous Hindu value of non judgement and love for all he wondered?

Max was only semi relieved when the final chant was over and students began getting up and filing out to the dining room downstairs. The Guru always offered hot lemongrass and ginger tea after class with a generous portion of fruits from the ashram's garden as a treat for the strenuous workout. It was a great time to socialize and he had a lot of memories of making new friends at these gatherings. Everyone was in a higher state of consciousness, with an open heart and mind and conversations flowed easily.

In this mindset, Max knew he was as ready as he would ever be. He would have to be. Dori looked more beautiful than he remembered from their short time together at the airport. Maybe it was the great yoga outfit or maybe it was the after yoga calm on her face. Whatever it was, he wished she was by herself. Fleur also looked great. Her smile was wide and bright and she walked with Dori without a trace of uneasiness. Good to be young, he thought to himself. The two women were walking towards him and closing in fast.

"Hello Max. Surprise! Dori said, with Fleur right next to her. "And I believe you know my friend, Fleur?"

"Skipping the niceties and cordial good mornings, are we?" he replied looking directly at Dori and Fleur. He had no idea how this would all unfold, but he had decided before entering the class that he would meet this whole thing head on. He had done nothing to feel bad about and he wasn't going to act like he had.

"No one is skipping anything," Dori answered back directly.

"That's pretty darn obvious. I guess a great yoga class can only do so much," Max countered.

"So you thought a great yoga class would make me feel better about flying to Bali to find you enjoying a little romance with someone more than half your age younger than you? It's been two days. That's pretty fast work. I'll give you that."

"This was a great yoga class," Fleur threw in quickly to see if she could stem the tide. "I had a great time. Thank you, Max."

"Thank you, Fleur. I'm sorry…"

"You're apologizing to Fleur", Dori said hastily.

"You didn't let me finish. I'm apologizing to both of you for this completely strange collision between us all. I had no intention to make anyone feel uncomfortable or angry or anything else."

"Max, my handsome friend," the Guru said as he joined the conversation. So good to see you again. You are the oldest man in class and as usual, you work hard the whole two hours. Then, after class, I find you surrounded by beautiful young women. I am jealous."

"Hello Guru," Max replied smiling. "Thank you for class today. It was really great."

"Are you going to introduce me to your friends?"

"I would like to, yes. This is Dori, on my left, and Fleur standing next to her."

The Guru took the hands of Dori and Fleur and gave them each a warm embrace. He then took their hands together in-between his two palms. "The sound travels to all corners of this room. This is our healing space and a place for love and forgiveness without judgement. Whatever troubles you, it is insignificant. It is only important how you treat each other now and moving forward. Please come downstairs for tea and cake. You are my guests."

"Thank you, Guru. I'll be down in a minute."

The guru smiled his knowing smile, and walked down the stairs to the dining area where the class meets after their workout.

Max looked at Dori and Fleur. Fleur was smiling and calm and Dori's emotions seemed to have calmed down as well. Her face looked at ease and her posture relaxed. He felt hopeful once again.

"He's a pretty interesting guy," Max said. "He loves you," Dori said back to him. "You're a very lucky man to have such a friend. I'm sorry I came at you right here in the yoga room."

"Let's get out of here," Max proposed. He took a few steps towards the staircase and the girls followed alongside him.

"So, Fleur. I hear your room is right next to Dori's. There are twenty empty rooms here. How did that even happen?"

"Can you imagine," Fleur said in her delightfully French way?"

"Never in a million years. So, I guess you two got to know each other a little?" Max was fishing for any possible hint that Fleur kept some aspects of their night together to herself.

The three of them looked at each other for a moment, until Dori broke the ice once again. "I guess it was meant to be, Max. I was honestly beginning to wonder if I was going to see you here at all until I met Fleur. I'm glad you weren't too tired for yoga."

There was silence once again. Max's cheeks burned red with that one. His mouth opened, but he struggled for a reply. He knew Fleur probably didn't have to actually speak the words for Dori to know they shared an intimate night.

"I'm teasing you," Max Dori said softly. I'm sorry. It was just right there and I couldn't hold it in.

"Are you done?"

"Yes, I'm done now, I swear. I promised Fleur I wouldn't be too hard on you. But damn, I think I'm entitled to a shot or two. I changed my ticket, flew to Bali, and no Max. But she did tell me how much you hoped I would be here. Was that for maybe a threesome?"

"Hey. No. No way. I thought you said you were done?"

"What? You would not want to have a threesome with me?" Fleur chided. She could not keep a straight face. To her it was all good. Life, sex, friends. The more the better. No one on their death bed ever said they wished they didn't have so much sex.

"Dori, now you?" Max asked in a friendly protest. "You're killing me here. Can we all go to the dining room? Let's have some tea, hang out, and you can ask me anything. Okay?"

With an impeccable sense of timing and a feeling of empathy for Max, Fluer jumped in to excuse herself and maybe save the day.

"Max, thank you so much for everything. You are so easy to tease. Everything is okay. Trust me. I told Dori if she is not nice to you, she is not invited to Paris." Fleur smiled and kissed Max on the cheek and continued. "I loved this class, and I love you for getting me a room. It was so kind of you. You saved my ass." Fleur moved over to Dori and put her arms around her for a hug and a kiss before she continued. "I'm also happy to meet you, my beautiful new friend. It was an interesting way to meet someone, but I hope we become friends. You are awesome. Now, I'm going into town. You two have some catching up to do. Maybe tomorrow we can all do something together, okay?"

Fleur gave Max another quick kiss on both cheeks and then did the same to Dori. After she kissed Dori she whispered something in her ear that made her smile.

"Au revoir Max and Dori. You look good together. S'amuser". (have fun) Shopping later?" she asked looking at Dori.

"Ciao," Dori replied to Fleur. "Porte toi bien a bientôt (have fun, see you soon) as Max looked on. See you later."

Fleur walked off to do her own thing and Max looked at Dori with a bit of wonderment and curiosity. "You speak French?" "Oui, Oui Max. She's a darling girl, isn't she?"

Max was at a loss for where to go next. Dori looked amazing. So did Fleur. She was so young and he really liked being with her in the time they shared, but that was the extent of it. Dori offered the hope of a true relationship in so many ways and he hoped they could move forward.

"So, should we go into town or maybe take a drive to the holy water site?" Max asked Dori.

"Can you give me a minute? I'm going to shower and change and then I'm going to let you take me to one of those amazing restaurants you were telling me about. Reception desk in an hour?"

"That sounds perfect. See you in an hour." Max beamed.

Max was relieved to escape the room with the promise of a lunch that he hoped would soothe things over. It wasn't as bad as it could've been, and he knew in his heart that the Guru and Fleur had something to do with that. Heck, she owed him that much. Why did she have to be crying at the registration desk up in the mountains just as he walked by? Enough of that, Max said to himself. The universe could be darn right troublesome at times.

CHAPTER SEVENTEEN

LUNCH WITH DORI

Max was as nervous as a high school senior getting ready for his first prom as he made his way towards the reception area for the shuttle into town. The long hot shower he took after yoga class helped a little, but he couldn't stop himself from wondering how Dori really felt about his brief encounter with Fleur.

He also gathered that Fleur and Dori had time to talk and there was no telling what details were explored, but he knew it was best to assume there was full disclosure. He hoped at least a few details were left out. He didn't cheat, he didn't do anything wrong, but he had a feeling he had something to prove and little time to prove it in.

Max felt hopeful when he saw Dori walking towards him. She was smiling, and wearing a beautiful flowered blue and white halter top with white cotton yoga style pants that stopped just above her sandals. It was simple and elegant, which was the perfect way to describe Dori. He remembered her amazing smile from their first meeting, but seeing her in a casual comfortable outfit that she would probably wear at home, shed a whole new perspective.

He could not take his eyes off her. A tan colored, wide brimmed summer hat complimented her perfectly. As she passed the pool, Max knew he was looking at a beautiful woman who would be turning heads whether walking the promenade along the shores of a Malibu beach, or the Champ Elysees in Paris.

"Hi Max. Did you decide on a place to eat? I'm famished."

"Yep. Clear Cafe in Ubud. It's in the heart of town and at this time of day it will be quiet enough to talk. Just so you know, before I went up to the mountains I made plans for things to do with you in case you showed up. I hope that's still an option."

"And alternate plans in case I didn't?" Dori said with a devilish grin.

"The shuttle is ready," Govinda said. "Are you joining?"

"Yes, Govinda. Just a minute." Max looked at Dori, put his arm out for her to grab to help her into the van. To his relief, before they stepped into the shuttle, Dori moved in with open arms and pulled him into her for a very sweet and affectionate hug.

"Thank you for setting things up for me, Max. It was great to have a hotel near the airport that first night after all that flight time. Your friend Wayan was there to pick me up in the morning and bring me here to Om Ham. It was really nice of you and made me feel important."

"You are important to me, Dori. I was an idiot for not getting your contact info. I would have stayed right here and taken the ride to the airport myself to get you in person."

"It's okay. Who knew, right?" I had no idea I would be here right up to boarding time. I'm glad you went up to the mountains to unwind from things. Well, not entirely glad."

"Well, this will be one great story to tell, right? I'd rather have a bad start and a great ending than the vice versa. What do you say to a drink and a toast to an amazing adventure together?"

"I'm ready if you are," she said with a big smile.

Max kissed her as close to her lips as possible without landing on them directly. He wanted to kiss her, to really kiss her, but considering the awkwardness of the Fleur encounter, he felt like this was a good time to go slow and let things heat up on their own. He hoped that was still on the table. Or bed.

The shuttle took its usual path towards the town center, and along the way, Max proudly pointed out the various landmarks Dori could use on her own adventures. One such gem was The Double AA Juicery. It looked more like someone's front porch back home, but inside there were two sisters who made the most delicious fresh juice drinks and smoothies in all of Ubud. They served breakfast as well, and if you saw the plates of food being placed on the tables, you wouldn't go anywhere else.

Another was the home of the now famous EAT LOVE PRAY healer, Wayan. The front of her home was decorated with a big poster from the movie, and she had no problem using it to earn a living. It was her father who sat with Julia Roberts in that famous scene where he looks at her palms and tells her she needs to have sex with a kind man who will soon come into her life.

She became friends with this man and he is still alive today, helping his daughter Wayan carry on the healing practice he started so many years earlier. And with perfect timing, just as Max and Dori passed by the house, there was a long line of men and women waiting to get inside to see her. Some were there to get a diagnosis of sorts, but for the most part, it was just another Bali experience and a story to tell when you got back home.

The Om Ham and Ubud Aura Shuttle finally came to a stop in front of their healing spa and massage center. It was the drop off and pick up spot for the two hotels, and it didn't hurt the business opportunities having guests dropped right in front of the best massage and healing center in Ubud - BODYWORKS.

Bodyworks is the home of Guru Ketut Arsana and his family, from his one hundred and two year old father to his newest nephew, only a few months old. It was where the guru taught his master yoga classes and held his healing sessions. There are many stories of his magical hands from Jakarta to Ubud and if you are lucky enough to get an appointment with him you will have your own story to tell. One of the trending stories was how he massaged the palms of his hands over the belly of a pregnant woman in order to move her baby from the painful legs first position to the natural head first posture for delivery.

He rarely accepted a fee and considered it his duty to his own people. His healing room at the ashram across from Om Ham was always filled with local men and women who needed his help either physically or spiritually. He had no problem, however, charging tourists a fair rate for his healing hands. Other than the yoga and massage rooms, the rest of the Bodyworks environment was landscaped with a combination of Koi fish ponds and intricate gardens. Beautiful years old artwork was painted or hung on the walls. It was truly a place to find and heal yourself if you were up to the task.

While Dori's head moved from side to side checking out this urban network of arts and crafts, food and healing services, Max led them forward to one of his favorite restaurants, Clear Cafe. A young Balinese host, Kadek, greeted them as they were removing their shoes to place on the floor near the entrance. Bali was not a place for the famous No Shirt, No Shoes, No Service signs that greet most diners as they enter a restaurant in America.

It was not uncommon to be in any of the casual restaurants and see young men shirtless and even young women sitting together holding hands. Whatever the cultural biases that existed in Indonesia as a whole, they were mostly ignored in Ubud. Ubud represented freedom to live your life peacefully and respectfully of others.

"Welcome to Clear Cafe. Here is the ticket for your shoes. Please come with me." Kadek handed Max a small paper and placed the matching side inside Max's shoes, and led them to a hostess station to be seated. Number 13! Off to a good start already, Max mused.

Dori had never seen a restaurant like this anywhere. There was a small canal, almost like a moat, that ran the length of the downstairs portion of the restaurant. Birds and fish of all colors and stripes made Clear Cafe feel like an outdoor restaurant in a nature preserve. Cameras were constantly flashing, and selfies over the Koi pond were as common as the photos of tourists pretending to hold up the leaning Tower of Pisa with their hands.

"This is amazing, Max. I've read stories and seen travel videos, but, of course, none of that compares to being here in person. Wow! It's really beautiful. Thank you."

"I'm glad you like it. The food is good and the drinks are really great."

"Are you ready for a table? Upstairs or downstairs?" the young hostess asked in perfect English.

"Downstairs by the water," Dori answered quickly. "Is that okay for you, Max?" "Perfect," he replied.

The hostess led them to a beautiful table just at the water's edge and placed menus in front of them. "Please enjoy," she said.

With drinks in their hands, Max put his next to Dori's and began his toast."

"To you, Dori, for good health and a happy adventure in Bali."

Dori tapped her glass to his and they each sipped. "Thank you again, Max. It's been a crazy couple of days and from the moment I landed at that insanely busy airport, it was easy to understand why Bali is on so many bucket lists."

"This is definitely bucket list territory. Personally, I don't believe in bucket lists. I believe in living life by doing what's important to you. I don't believe in living a life where you say, "one day I will do that". Most of the time, that one day never comes. All the times you could have done that very thing will have passed."

"You're an interesting man, Max."

"That's kind of you to say, and if it's okay with you, I would like to hear the Dori story. Your philosophy on life."

"Maybe. I guess that depends on what kind of story you are expecting to hear." Dori was a little surprised at herself. On the airplane and at the airport a week ago, she was ready to tell him whatever he asked, and now, after seeing him with another woman, she felt herself wanting to hold back a bit.

"Anything you want to share, Max offered. I want to get to know you while you're here. You know, what makes you happy? What about love drives you crazy? Why yoga in Thailand? Things like that."

"Can we not ignore the elephant in the room before we start chatting like we just left the airport?" Dori asked. She was gentle and non judgmental in her question, but she made her point. Neither of them could pretend that he did not just spend two days with a beautiful young woman.

Max felt the rush of blood to his cheeks. He knew he was blushing. He also knew he had to answer. "I don't want to ignore it. I'm here with *you*. I was hoping you would come from the moment we parted in Hong Kong. I was an idiot for not getting your email or some way to contact you.

"Yes you were. I could have also asked, but thank you for saying that, Dori offered. The tension eased and Max's eyebrow unfurled.

"You know, I did make plans in case you did come. They're on the books. The thing I didn't plan was meeting Fleur in the mountains. I hope you will stay. I want you to stay. You're the woman I want to be with." He said it. He said her name, he didn't back off and as hard it was, he felt better on the inside. Most of the knot in his stomach was gone. Now it was up to Dori.

Dori could feel his words getting to her. The wall she was building in her mind and the normal frustration of what happened between him and Fleur started to matter less. She believed what he was saying and was happy to hear him say it.

"After sitting at the cafe with you between our flights, I felt the same. I don't play games, Max." Dori took a breath, then continued.

"I want someone in my life who feels the same. I'd like to know what makes you happy as well. And I like that that's what you're interested in knowing about me. If we get to that point, there are personal aspects of my life I want to share with someone who is more than a casual fling. Maybe that will be you, Max."

Max was keeping calm, but he did feel a little defensive with that comment. It sounded unlike who he thought Dori really was. It also sounded mean.

"I don't want a casual fling either, Dori. Fleur was not a fling. She is sweet and funny, and she needed an ear and a shoulder at a tough moment in her life."

"Well, if it was only an ear and a shoulder," Dori injected sarcastically and with a smile.

"You sure you're not from Chicago? I was almost missing the sarcasm. Look, I'm not going to lie and say I didn't have a good time with her. It was honest and it was nice. And I'm a million years older than her which we laughed about. We're Friends. Period! I'm here with *you* now, and that's all that matters. That's all I want to matter. I can keep groveling if you want."

Like a hot knife through butter, the tension melted away. Soon, Max and Dori were digging into their food smiling and laughing and sharing stories of their travels. They were served traditional appetizers of Chinese style spring rolls, cups of pumpkin soup served with breaded garlic balls, and an American staple of sweet potato fries.

A local favorite, nasi goreng (mixed fried rice) baki (meatballs) and a side dish of sambal, which is a chili sauce made up of lots of different peppers and not for the faint of heart or sensitive tummy topped things off.

Their plates were mostly empty, and Max decided it was time to break the ice and get right at the heart of what he was thinking about most.

"So, Dori… I have to ask you. What made you change your flight to Bali? Did you change your mind about the yoga course in Thailand?"

"No. I'm still going. It starts in eight more days. I was planning on coming to Bali afterwards, and I just thought, well… here is this nice man I met, he's from California, and he might not be there after my yoga program. So take a chance I told myself. And here I am."

"That's a very spontaneous move. And brave. I'd like to believe I could do that if the opportunity presented itself. I know one thing…"

"And what might that be?" Dori posed.

"If there was a chance at love with a beautiful woman, who looked at life as I do, I would do anything in my power to make it happen. In a heartbeat. That doesn't sound too desperate, does it," he asked hopefully?

"Not at all. It sounds romantic. I'd like to believe that all of us want that one great love in our lifetime. The one that takes away our fear and doubts about everything else as long as we love each other."

Dori was a romantic. Even though his mind was way ahead of his words, he felt relieved. He was getting aroused looking at his beautiful new friend. She was funny, sweet, and he loved the sound of her voice, the smell of her hair and her easy way. Her breasts were pushing freely against her white halter top and it was difficult to avoid looking a little lower than is considered polite when talking to a woman.

Max could only laugh at himself when he remembered his futile days as a teenager playing at the game of love. The jocks, the playboys of the school, were chased enough by all the prettiest girls and they soon learned how to reach under a blouse, pinch quickly and be cupping bare skin before much of a protest could be lodged.

He struggled through, saved by the "Burn the Bra" revolution of the sixties and the few women kind enough to put him out of his misery by unsnapping those darn things for him.

"I have a question for you, Mr. Max. Why Bali? What makes a country so far from America and so opposite to the way of life most Americans aspire to, your choice to call home?"

"Do you believe in signs or unexplainable coincidences?" Max asked. "I'm all ears," Dori replied.

"Well, for one, and it's a big one, my birthday of August seventeenth, is Indonesian Independence Day. I mean, how's that for starters? It helped me understand that little feeling of being emotionally tied to this place. It made me feel connected. Like it was meant to be.

"Go on".

"All righty. If you insist. For at least five years before I took my first trip to Bali, I had books on Bali all over my house. Coffee table books, history books, the incredible beaches. Something was always pulling me there until one day my first trip became possible. Once I got back to Los Angeles, all I could think about was when I could get back. On my third trip, I knew I was only coming back to LA to sell all my things and get the longest visa I could. It felt like a calling. Even better, I have never had even a sniffles or cold or felt anything but healthy and happy here. This is home."

"It sounds like you found your happy place and acted on it. Not many people can say that or do what they know in their heart is what they really want."

"It's good, thank you. I wish it didn't take me fifty years to find it," he said laughing.

There was something else on Dori's mind, but she decided she would let this sweet day play itself out. There would be time later to get more answers. "How about we get out of here and go get that great desert you mentioned? I have a little room left for something sweet."

Max and Dori were still wiping traces of Takut's fresh coconut ice cream from their lips when the shuttle parked in the Om Ham driveway. They got out with a few other guests and walked together towards their rooms. He did not have long to work up the courage he hoped would present itself in the next hundred feet. As the last possible opportunity arrived, Max smiled his best hopeful and happy smile.

"Dori, would you like to come in?"

Dori was caught off guard, but not by much. She noticed how Max looked at her during their meal, and even way back at the airport when he turned to tell her where she could find him. She was free, happy and single, but not sure if she was ready for more than what seemed like an easy, fun friendship, at least with him. At least so far. Remnants of his tryst with Fleur were still knocking around in her head. It was also their first day together and she still had questions. Her heart wanted to say yes. Her mind wanted more time.

"Thank you, Max. Actually, Fleur and I are going to meet at the reception area in a couple of hours. Your friend Wayan is going to take us for a sunset dip in the healing waters of Tirta Empul."

Max stayed quiet, choosing discretion over valor.

"That's not a problem is it?" Dori asked.

"No, of course not. It's a great experience. I'll see you around, then. Have a great time."

"It's just a girls day kind of thing. We actually talked about it before the subject of a particular older man she met up in the mountains even came up."

"I see. So now I'm the older man?" Max asked.

"You are to her, that's for sure," Dori said laughing.

"Gee, thanks a lot."

"I'm teasing, Max. And you may have to put up with it for a little while. Can you handle it?" Dori said with a sweet smile.

"I can handle it."

"Good. I had a great time with you today. I'll see you later, okay? Maybe try and stay up past 8:00!"

"You're a funny girl. I'll go take a long nap and maybe get some anti-aging herbs from the guru's garden."

"Perfect. See you later." With that, Dori was on her way to an adventure with Fleur.

Max was dejected, but not surprised and he hoped he didn't over react. He hid it as well as he could and walked into his room. It had been a long time since he was on a real date and he didn't want it to end. He was never good at playing cat and mouse, and always believed things would work out best if he could be straightforward and honest about his feelings in all of his relationships, men or women.

As hard as he tried, his thoughts couldn't escape him. He wanted to take Dori in his arms and let nature and chemistry take things on a sweet, wild ride. He wanted to know every inch of her body and make love to her until they each collapsed on the bed exhausted from pushing the pleasures of the flesh to its limits. For now, he would have to settle for some mantras and a nap.

CHAPTER EIGHTEEN

FLEUR AND DORI

ayan's white van stopped at the main gate for the girls to get out. It was a newer Toyota which he took great pride in. He had two sons in school and a wife at home to support all on a salary of thirty to forty dollars a day when business was good. He kept his van sparkling clean and had his business logo painted on each side- Wayan's Temple Tours on one side, and Explore Bali Life on the other. He was always courteous and appreciative that Max gave out his cards and promoted his business and he took extra great care to make sure Max's friends enjoyed their time in Bali.

"Wait for me here, you need a Bali guide to enter. I go park."

"Thank you, Wayan," the girls said together.

Wayan returned shortly and he walked the girls to the first stop, a small tent where the admission price was paid and the Holy Water Temple sarongs were handed to the girls along with a locker key. They had to wear proper ceremonial attire as well as a white T-shirt over their bathing suits for the sake of modesty in the cold water. Not a bad price to get cleansed in holy water.

The locker room was very spartan in nature. There were rows of lockers on each side of a wide cement floor, and a separate shower area with small nozzles designating each space. There were no hot and cold knobs to turn. You got what came out.

Wayan led the two women from the locker room to the holy water pool. He held a big towel for each of them and told them about the various statues of the Hindu Gods placed around the pool from end to end and what kind of prayers were usually said. It was common to pray for good health and prosperity and to keep negative energy away. He also told the girls to keep moving from statue to statue. The ritual was done three times around the pool and then you exit at the shallow end and dry off on the steps.

"This is pretty, cool, don't you think?" Fleur asked as she and Dori walked to the first statue.

"I'm ready if you are. Do you know what you are going to say?"

"I'm going to say a few prayers for my dad, and for my mom and sister back home. After that, I'm going to just see what comes out."

It seemed like Fleur was ready and eager for this kind of setting to let out some of the many thoughts about how her dad's death was affecting her and her family. Dori had her own worries and personal issues to ask for help with; issues she had yet to share with Max. She wanted to ask for the ability to see things clearly, keep negative people and energy away, and to bring good health and prosperity into her life.

Dori nodded and they began their slow walk through the cold water with about one hundred other men, women and children all wading in to get cleansed. For the Balinese people, it was not unusual to come two or three times per week. Prayer was the dominant aspect of their lives at home and any other place on the island the statues of their gods were present.

Wayan brought his cooler to the park-like area near the entrance and told the girls to meet him there after they handed in their sarongs. He passed around mangos, home grown bananas, and bottled water. While they ate and drank he gave the girls a short history lesson of the temple. He was a first class guide and his excellent English and knowledge of all the local customs made him a sought after driver for all the different cultural experiences available.

The girls were thankful and let him know they would be sure to spread the word. Wayan loved to hear such a great compliment, as his living depended on word of mouth and the generosity of Western tourists. The sunset ride back to Om Ham gave the girls a good chance to talk about their experience and their lives.

"Are you still angry with me?"Fleur asked.

"You're too cute to be mad at, at least for very long," Dori laughed. And sweet. Honestly, I wasn't really mad, I was jealous. I thought I was past that kind of reaction, but there you go. Outdone by a pretty French girl."

Fleur was giggling that sweet, easy laugh of a young woman at ease with herself. "Dori, You're so beautiful. I'm the one who is jealous. You are smart and sexy, and if I didn't know you are here for Max, I might be hitting on *you*."

"You might not have to try so hard," Dori shot back. "Between you and Max and me, I'm the only one here not getting any love."

"You will be together. He talked about you a lot when we walked through the town. Dori is this and Dori is doing yoga in Thailand. He's very into you."

Dori felt her cheeks flush and any remnants of jealousy she had about Fleur and Max just dissolved like sugar in hot water. "Thank you, Fleur. I feel a lot better now. I didn't know what to make of it all at first, but I'm good. We meet who we meet and sometimes, some pretty interesting shit happens for a reason. At least that's what I've been told," Dori said laughing.

"The holy water is working already," Fleur chimed in.

"If it were that simple I would come here every day, Dori added. Let' all do something tomorrow. Max told me about this amazing place, The Pyramids of Chi. It's a sound healing sanctuary and has a cafe and gardens. What do you think?"

The tour van pulled under the arch leading into Om Ham and the girls jumped out putting a nice tip in Wayan's hand and waving goodbye as he drove off.

"I would love to," Fleur answered. "I'm going up to my room and call my mom. I can feel her walking around here with me."

Dori gave Fleur a hug and a kiss. "You're a good girl, Fleur. Your mom will love to hear from you."

Dori walked off to the Tulsi dining room as Fleur walked up to her room. She wasn't quite ready to go to her room after such a unique and amazing experience at the temple, so she sat down and ordered a pot of relaxing tulsi tea. Dori never heard of tulsi tea and was surprised and happy to learn about all the natural benefits to drinking it. It's very popular in Ayurvedic healing diets, and is a natural herb that helps the body adapt to outside stressors. It also helps maintain the level of the cortisol hormone in the body, which is known as the stress hormone. Not bad, she thought. It was soothing and relaxing and even lowers the level of blood sugar. Even better, she learned she could walk across the street to the ashram and pick some to make in her room.

Her teapot arrived and while she sipped, she wondered if she should go to Max's room and maybe hang out, or just stop by to say hi. She still carried the original feelings she had for him from their first meeting, but she couldn't help feeling a bit more caution than usual. She was also a girl who appreciated the safety, sexiness and no strings hassle of a sweet vacation romance. The inner conflicts a woman must deal with she thought as she walked to his room.

"Knock, knock" Dori said as she gently tapped on Max's door. She could hear the Krishna Das sound track Rahde Govinda playing in the background and it made her smile. She liked that his life was fairly simple from what she gathered. He was not caught up in what's hip or popular or cool, or in keeping up with what anyone else is doing.

He was comfortable in his own skin and seemed genuinely happy when on his own. Big points for that. Max opened the door in his knee length yoga pants and tan linen buttoned V-neck pullover. It was the kind where the buttons just go from the neck down to mid chest. He wore it with the buttons open, his white chest hair looking sexy against the black beads he used for meditation.

Dori stood half in his room and half on the tiled hallways of the corridor. She looked him over, liking what she saw. Each time she saw him, she had that same jelly belly feeling in her stomach. It was butterflies bouncing and she could not pretend otherwise regardless of what happened or how hard she tried.

Max looked affectionately at her as she stood half in and half out of his room. "Well…come on…all the way would be nice."

"Hold onto your beads there, mister," she joked as she came all the way in and closed the door behind. Her hair was still a little wet, and had natural curls at the bottom just past her shoulders. She was in a silky blouse that was open over her bikini top and the white yoga pants she left in. She felt sexy and sensual and liked to dress that way. It was for her, but she appreciated the way Max looked at her every time he saw her.

"You look… very clean," Max said smiling. How was the holy water?"

"Cold and crowded, Dori answered. I'll know more later, right?"

"Maybe. I had some strange and very vivid dreams for a couple of nights after my dip. I enjoyed it."

"Anyway,I just wanted to say hi. We had a great time and I'm actually starting to feel the effects of the long day and the big pot of tea I just had. Fleur and I are going to the Pyramids of Chi tomorrow and we would like you to join us. If you want to."

"I would love to. That's one of my favorite places on the island that isn't food. Thank you. Does the 11:00 A.M. session good?"

"Perfect. See you in the morning, Max. Good night." "Sweet dreams, Dori."

Dori pulled the door closed behind her and walked away and up the stairs to her room. Max just sat on the edge of his bed alone with his thoughts. Relax, he said to himself. Tomorrow would come soon enough and he was much happier now then when the girls took off together without him earlier in the day.

Dori looked beautiful and it felt like she was ready to get to know him and let go of the Fleur thing. He sure was. Nothing like feeling that you may have lost someone to make you want them more. Coffee together at the Hong Kong airport was only a week ago and his feelings shifted from it being a nice way to kill a few hours to wondering if he met the woman he had been hoping would find him. Time will tell, he always says.

CHAPTER NINETEEN

FLEUR SAYS GOOD BYE

Fleur arrived at the reception area in a light pink, short summer mini dress and white sandals. She had on a tortoise shell necklace against a low neckline showing off a great tan that brought all eyes in her direction. With no extra effort on her part, she was a perpetual tease. She slipped off her backpack and shopping bag of gifts for her mom and sister and gave it all to Govinda to watch for a few hours. She signed up for the quick shuttle to the Pyramids and added Max and Dori to the list. Govinda smiled and gladly took her bags for safekeeping and gave her three coupons for free drinks at the Pyramids Cafe. "These are for you. The shuttle leaves in ten minutes. Should I call the room for Max and Dori?"

Before Fleur could answer, Dori was waving hello from the balcony of her room. "Two minutes," she called out, holding up two fingers to remove all doubt. Fleur and Govinda laughed and just a few seconds later, Max arrived to make sure he was in on the party.

"Good morning, everyone, he announced. He was happy and his smile was all the evidence needed. Is Dori coming?"

"Two minutes she said," Fleur answered.

Dori was in shouting distance and heard Fleur's reply. "Give a girl a minute, will ya?" She met up with her friends and not to be outdone by Fleur, she was decked out in camouflage print

Lululemon yoga pants, a dark gray mid tummy t-shirt, and beach style sandals with flower emblems on the top straps. Max looked on approvingly, and felt pretty darn good about being able to walk into the pyramids reception area with two beautiful women.

"Everybody in, Govinda called out."

Udi was the driver today and had the engine running with the AC turned on high. It was an unusually hot, humid day and it was nice to enjoy a cool ride. It was one thing to sit in 85 degree heat with 80% humidity while next to a swimming pool and another altogether while walking the bumpy broken sidewalks of Ubud. It was a good thing there were so many massage places, Max thought to himself. It was hard to walk a few blocks without missing a step and finding your back and hips in need of attention.

It wasn't uncommon to hear tourists at their restaurant tables comparing notes on where they got the best massage. It was easy. The best massage was everywhere and anywhere you could find an empty Easy Boy recliner to lie back in. Govinda opened the door and Max and the girls got in for the short ten minute drive.

"Ready for some great gong sounds," Max said to Dori and Fleur?

"I think we are, Max. Especially, if it's as good as you've been saying. I mean, how much preparation do you need to lie down and close your eyes," she said with her best teasing smile. Dori was happy and energetic and excited for their group outing.

"I see the Holy Water hasn't improved your sense of humor yet, Max threw back. You'll see soon enough. It's a tourist attraction for sure, but it's also a regular spot for a lot of the locals and expats. Healing is healing. There's an amazing garden to walk around in if you're not ready for people yet, and the deserts at the cafe are pretty darn good as well."

"Speaking of deserts, Govinda gave me coupons for free drinks or food. I could use one already, Fleur added."

"Me too. I didn't make my coffee this morning. I could use a hot vanilla latte'. You know, just to get things moving."

"Isn't there a chant for that," Dori said teasing?

"What's going on here? Are you girls working on a routine or something? Thankfully, there's no talking once we get inside the sound room."

Fleur was going to wait to break the news of her imminent departure after the sound bath, but this seemed like the perfect moment.

"You know, I'm going to really miss listening to you two and watching the way you smile when you're together. You sound like best friends already. I'm going to miss hanging out with both of you when I'm gone."

"Gone where?" Max asked.

The van came to a stop under a large canopy that served as a carport just as Fleur was about to answer.

"Everybody out. Udi opened the doors and helped Fleur and Dori down. See you all in two hours. If you decide to take the Pyramid shuttle into town, we can pick you up at the Bodyworks stop. Good?"

Max reached into his pocket and pulled out a fifty thousand dollar note for Udi. "Very good, Udi. This is for you. See you later." "Thank you, Mr. Max."

Everyone did the quick, polite forward bow with palms together, and Udi drove off with the cash in his shirt pocket. It was only three dollars to Americans, but for Udi, it was enough to bring home a big plate of food from one of the local warungs.

Two huge white tents in the exact shape as the famous pyramids of ancient Egypt were just a few hundred yards to their left as they got out of the van. The entrance into the main building was a guided tile walkway with colorful bushes and flower pots leading to the front doors. Humming birds hummed above at the scattered feeders, and other colorful birds danced just above them enjoying the peaceful energy that served all.

Inside was even more spectacular. The thirty foot high wood beam ceilings gave the feeling of being outdoors. There were skylights and windows in every direction. In the center of the lobby a few rows of chairs and sofas were designated for sitting and relaxing with bistro tables and menus. Off against one wall, there was a large collection of gift items like prayer beads, crystals for wearing or holding in your pocket and small books on the history of the pyramids, yoga in Bali, and the magic of the healing that goes on in the sanctuary.

"This is gorgeous, Max. Thank you. I would have missed this for sure in my short time here," Dori said.

"Me too, Max. Thank you. You are a good guide. If you ever need a job here, you can work with Wayan," Fleur said laughing at her own joke.

"Yes, well, you never know, do you?" Max replied. " Maybe I *will* be here long enough to need a job. If I am, I hope I can be lucky enough to help you both explore more of the island."

"That was sweet, Max. Very sweet." Dori took his hand in hers and pulled him close for a kiss on the cheek.

A voice over the loudspeaker interrupted their chatter telling the room that the first session was going to begin in twenty minutes. It was time to pay at the registration desk and get your free eye pillow to help you immerse yourself in the sounds.

A tall man, at least six foot three or four, dressed in all white with a tan fisherman's hat and a leather man purse over his left shoulder appeared at the registration desk. He introduced himself with only his first name, Paul.

His voice was deep and resonating and made every word he said sound believable. It didn't hurt that he had a heavy Australian accent. He was the owner and builder of the Pyramids of Chi and gave everyone a brief description of what was going to happen. He had told this story many times before and he had the well practiced humor of a tour guide on a chartered bus in Italy.

The buzzing in the line to enter the pyramids stopped the moment you were inside the room. It was dark inside, the only light being what filtered in through the tent like walls of the pyramid. In the center of the room, two huge golden gongs held in place by their wooden support beams drew all the attention as the guests filed in. There were rows of foam beds covered with sheets and folded blankets at the side of each one. It wasn't unusual for people to rush for the beds closest to the gongs, but in reality, the closer you were to the back or side walls, the more sound you actually received. The gong, when hit with precision and power, would send deep resonating sound waves that would bounce off all the solid objects in the room and fill the space with their magical vibrations.

Just one solid tap by a professional gong player and the sound would carry for a few minutes at a time, building in strength until it faded out. With eyes closed and mind at ease, these healing sounds could take a person on a very interesting journey. It was common for people into lucid dreaming and astral travel to have some incredibly metaphysical experiences while under the spell of the gong master.

As Max looked around waiting to be angelically guided to a bed, he remembered his last experience at the Pyramids. The gong players come on a rotating basis and each has his or her own specialty. They play the gong only half the time. The second half can be some other form of sound healing which is up to the guest player. It usually includes flutes, wind chimes, rain-sticks, etc. It was never anything that detracted from his experience.

The gong started out with the usual soft taps building slowly until they became louder and longer lasting in intensity. Max most often fell into a deep sleep, waking up just a few minutes before the session was about to end. He never knew where he went specifically while his eyes were closed, but when he woke, he knew he traveled somewhere. His mind was quiet, his body fully at rest. This one time, however, was one he would never forget for a much different reason.

In a deep sleep, he was awakened by loud war cries of an American Indian. The sounds were unmistakable for any kid who ever watched an American Western involving cowboys and Indians. Max sat upright in his bed. He looked around and noticed all the other guests being very still, either lying down or sitting in yoga pose with their hands on their knees.

In the center of the room, the gong player was now dressed in an Indian Chief headdress and he was crying in deep, loud tones of pain and hurt that seemed to go on forever. For Max, it was panic time. The war cries must have touched a nerve he never knew he had. It was some kind of emotional trigger and the only thing he could do was get up quietly and then run out of the room to the main building. He found an empty sofa and sat down. The owner of the pyramids noticed him and approached.

"Sir, are you okay? Your eyes look very distant."

"I don't know," Max said in a shaky voice. "I'm kind of freaked out to be honest with you. I felt like I was at an Indian massacre in the days of the wild west."

The owner, Paul, the man in the all white outfit, sat down and ordered a pot of tea and cookies and explained about emotional triggers that can happen at such an event. He apologized if it was a painful experience and offered him a free lunch and a return visit. Max was okay with the free lunch, but at the moment, a return visit seemed unlikely. But, time and being with two beautiful women had him here once again. Who could have guessed?

Max, Dori and Fleur found beds to their liking. Fleur and Dori chose beds next to each other, and Max, thinking of his last visit, picked a spot on the opposite side. If he was going to freak out again, he didn't want Dori and Fleur to see it. Once everyone was settled on their bed, an announcement was made and the guest player entered the room. This day, it was Punu, an Indian mystic, Reiki Master and astrologer of sixty or seventy years. It was hard to tell. He was wearing a white turban and ceremonial Seek attire. When the room was completely silent, he introduced himself very briefly and then hit the gong. Show on.

An hour later, the guests were moving slowly and silently out the door to either the main building or the lush gardens off to the other side. Max was out first, and as he sat on the bench putting his sandals on, the girls came out together and sat next to him. Dori and Fleur put their sandals on and all three sat there silently for a moment.

"I'd like to walk through the gardens. I'm not quite ready to be around people, Dori said very softly. Is that okay with you guys?"

"I feel the same, Fleur said. But, as I was saying earlier, I'm afraid I have to say goodbye to you both. I'm heading to the airport."

Fleur had tears dropping slowly down the side of her face. "I'm so happy to meet you both. I love you. I hope I see you again. And don't say, you never know, Max."

Dori gave Fleur a long, tight hug and a sweet kiss as she held both of her hands in hers. "Au revoir mon cher ami."

"Can I get in there?" Max moved in between the girls and gave Fleur a sweet kiss and warm, loving hug. What was between them was genuine and it showed in their embrace.

"Take care of yourself, Fleur. Thank you for ruining your credit card." They all laughed and hugged quickly one last time before Fleur walked to her waiting taxi.

Dori reached over and took Max's hand in hers. "Shall we stroll through the gardens?"

Max didn't say anything. He just held Dori's hand and started walking with her. The path was narrow, with wooden and brick steps surrounded on both sides by the lush flora of Indonesia, and Bali in particular. Dandelion, fennel and huge patches of lemongrass provided free aroma therapy along with the shade and mysticism of the leafy banyan trees.

Banyan trees are native to the Indian subcontinent as well as labeled as the National Tree of India. They reach a height of up to one hundred feet and will spread laterally indefinitely if not cared for and manicured occasionally. At least that's what the plaque stapled to their bench said. There were benches perfectly placed along the path to sit and enjoy all the gifts of the garden. It was a special place to be still and let the healing effects of the gongs work their magic. Max and Dori sat in silence until the sun started to drop behind the mountains in the distance.

FIRES BURNING

Sometimes a day just comes to an end with nothing more to say to the people you spent it with. Max, Dori, and Fleur shared a lot in their short time together. It was emotional, funny and sweet and gave each of them insights into their own sense of well being and purpose. This was what Bali meant to him. Max never met a person who did not affect him in a real way, one way or another. It seemed everyone was who was in Bali had a story to tell and was there to find a new direction or purpose in life.

He thought about the time he met a slightly younger man than he in a little boutique on Monkey Forest Road when they both reached for the same shirt. They were only talking for a few minutes when Max mentioned he had been in Bali for three months and was feeling like he was ready to go back to California.

"Why on earth would you do that," the man said with a look of disbelief in his eyes? "It takes that fucking long to learn where to eat and find your comfort zone." He spoke with a Londoner's accent and wore a dark blue turban around his head. He had such a look of confidence and inner presence, Max wanted to hear all he had to say.

The man introduced himself as Peter Singh and offered Max one of his cards. "Next time you have such a crazy thought, call me and we will have tea. I've been here five years, in case you were wondering." This story always made Max feel good about his days in Bali and that he was back there now. These are the kinds of stories and experiences he was looking forward to sharing with Dori if given the opportunity. There were so many, they could share a lifetime talking about them.

Max was happy to be back in his room. The day with Dori was one that, for him, brought them closer. As much as he enjoyed Fleur's attention and affection, he knew that was a *live in the moment* kind of thing. It was sweet and uplifting, and most of all it was honest and unpretentious. There was no jealousy or possessiveness and she was truly happy for him to have this time now, to be with Dori and find out what lies ahead, if anything.

He was at least honest enough with himself and his ego to know that Fleur was not thinking of him in any other way but as a good man who came into her life at a time she needed an older voice to listen to and hang out with. She lifted him out of a long lapse of sexual intimacy in a way he could never have imagined. It was a good story. His dear cousin Brad would have loved to hear about it.

As for the rest of his friends, they would have to read about it in his memoirs. For now, it was time to relax. He had a few favorite meditation gurus, and one in particular, Sadhguru, was his choice for this moment. He turned on his tablet, found a lesson on self awareness and manifesting desires and hit play. It was barely eight in the evening but he was in a very restful state before the first track finished playing.

Max was resting against the headboard in a loose long sleeve t-shirt, with his headphones on and his legs under the sheets, when he thought he heard a knock on his door. He waited a minute and after the second knock, he removed his headphones.

"It's open," he said, wondering who it could be.

Dori walked halfway in, and with the light of the full moon at her back, her silhouetted figure was a vision equal to any dream he ever had. She was wearing a long, sky blue Balinese style, thin summer ankle length dress with slits along the legs that went up to mid thigh and cut to a low neckline.

He had seen them on the mannequins in the store windows on Hanoman Street in Ubud. This was much better. The light of the full moon pouring through the ultra thin fabric wrapped around her legs offered as good a fantasy as any erotic film he ever watched.

"I have hot tea and a bottle of wine. You can choose when you come over. Twenty minutes work for you?" Dori's smile seemed filled with temptation and desire. Both felt like a perfect end to a perfect day.

"Yeah, yes Max said, clearing his throat and hoping he didn't sound like a sailor who just stepped onto dry land after six months of submarine duty. I'll be right there."

In barely a minute, Max was in his favorite bamboo yoga pants and long sleeve white T-shirt with an OM insignia on the front. His mind was racing, but in honor of men everywhere and to prove to himself he still had some semblance of self respect and manliness, he forced himself to wait another ten minutes before walking into Dori's room.

Pride goeth before the fall, someone once said. Max wasn't sure that even fit this situation, but he waited nonetheless. And at the moment, he didn't care a lick about pride.

Not that long ago, he would have rolled up a quick doobie to ease his nervousness and slow things down a bit. It always felt like the senses were enhanced with a puff or two. Food tasted better, music sounded better, and touch felt extra sensual. Doobies were a ritual to him. He would get out his bag of flowered herb, trim enough buds to roll the perfect joint, make his cup of coffee and retreat to a deck chair with a view. He used to brag that he could roll a perfect joint one handed while riding a horse.

Maybe doobie rolling was a great skill for that time in his life, but it was surely not one that made his mother proud. Thankfully, being in Bali for so long, where a quick doobie can land you in the harshest of prisons while awaiting a public hanging, Max pushed those thoughts out of his mind and learned how to settle for the occasional BinTang beer. For now, no mind, body, or mood enhancers were needed. He felt flushed with desire at his good fortune to be where he was.

When he finally walked into Dori's room, she was sitting in bed leaning on the pillows fluffed up against the back of the bed. She was half under the covers, wearing a silky orange night shirt that slid off her shoulders with only a robe style belt tied loosely at the waist keeping her from being totally exposed.

Soft jazz played on her laptop and lavender scented candles were burning on the two nightstands opposite the bed. A small tray with a bottle of wine and two glasses rested on the dresser near the door. She was a vision of beauty that he would never forget. And she was here for him. The lace curtains were drawn down and the onset of a typical rainy season thunderstorm provided the perfect romantic soundtrack and moody dark sky.

"You look so beautiful." "Pour us a glass of wine and come sit next to me," Dori said as she offered her hand out to Max.

Max poured the wine and gave one of the glasses to Dori.

"To new beginnings," Dori toasted. "To new beginnings," Max repeated. They tapped glasses and took a sip. Dori took two. Max kept it to one. He enjoyed wine, but didn't drink very much. It gave him a headache, and also affected his libido at this stage of life. He doubted that would hamper anything here and now. Dori had every inch of him excited about all the possibilities.

Max took the glass from her hand and put his and hers on the nightstand. He took her hand in his, sat down on the bed and rested his head on the pillow next to hers. He leaned in towards her to kiss her lips in what became a long sensual kiss they used to ease down flat onto the bed together.

The passion was mutual, and as Max moved from Dori's lips down the side of her neck, his right hand moved to Dori's waist where he untied the soft belt. He hesitated there for a moment. Dori's top was now off to the side, her bare breasts moving up and down with each breath waiting for his attention. He wanted this to happen and was equally surprised it was happening.

Dori moved her free hand under Max's chin and turned his face towards hers. "Maybe you should get under the covers with me," she suggested. Max agreed and got out of his clothes and slid under the covers next to her. Her skin was warm and soft and felt good against his body.

"I thought about you often today, Max. At the holy water and then sitting in the garden with you so quiet. There were no words and yet we fell into this space together where I wanted you to be here, now, for this. I feel like we should be together. Make love to me, Max."

Max started to say something and Dori put her hand against his lips, then kissed his lips and lowered his hands to her breasts. He cupped them firmly, swirling his fingers around her nipples. His kisses moved lower to cover Dori's full and round breasts with his mouth, alternating moments on each sweet nipple as they became hard and aroused. He felt calm and excited all at once, in no hurry to arrive at any particular destination. Dori's body responded as he hoped, moving slowly under him as her legs parted naturally.

Max's right hand moved slowly, massaging each breast, caressing, probing, twisting, pinching, then moving down the side of her leg stopping just below her hips with his hand resting between her legs against her inner thigh. He could feel the heat coming from her sex the closer he got to entering her.

He brushed slowly over her mound with his hand, and her wetness invited him in as he moved her thighs farther apart. In her arms, in the heat of passionate kisses, he slid one finger inside her wet pussy, moved it slowly in circles then deeper. Her hips moved up to meet his fingers so he inserted another, probing dark places with bodies arching and writhing. Everything before this moment faded.

Dori joined him in their mutual exploration and moved her hand between his thighs, feeling his cock for the first time, excited to feel it grow harder and taller in response to her touch. She sat up only for a moment, kissed Max on the lips, face, and eyelids and then back on his lips, rejoicing in being completely naked with him. She rolled over on top of him and let her hands take him gently inside her. She moved slowly, rocking forwards and back, sideways and back, mimicking one of her favorite yoga exercises which consists of rotating on the sit bone. It was sensual and their passion built together.

Max was deliriously happy. He wanted to be loved like this for so long. To have a woman hold his face between her hands, to love touching him as if there was nothing she would rather be doing or nowhere she would rather be. He wanted to know what love is and he wanted her to show him.

Dori was still on top, barely moving while feeling her pleasure come rushing to a climax. "Max", she whispered, not in search of an answer. Dori's breathing turned into a soft moan as her body quivered a few times as she released and fell off to the side and rested on her tummy with both hands on Max's chest. One of her legs was still between Max's legs as their breathing and heartbeats returned to a slower pace.

"Hey beautiful girl," Max whispered, not moving even an inch. Max put his hands on each side of Dori's neck and shoulder area, gently massaging her. "A massage too," she whispered?

"It's included. Shall I continue?" he said with a grin. Dori just nodded softly in approval. She loved his hands and that he had both a gentle yet confident way of touching her. He wasn't insecure about having her put his hands where she wanted them. Her tummy was still resting between Max's legs and her head was resting comfortably just below his neck.

She could feel him still aroused and occasionally pulsing against her inner thigh. He didn't cum, and she loved that it didn't matter to him. It turned her on even more. She took her right hand off his chest and reached behind her to take hold of him. She wrapped her long fingers around him gently, then pumped slowly, up and down, running her finger nails over the top and back down and then back up. Her touch was light and magical, alternating between barely touching his skin and squeezing at the right spot for just a moment.

She sensed when to stop, when to start, when to go fast and when to slow down. She felt his excitement, and abandoned any desires she may have had earlier. She felt free to do whatever came naturally and when she felt his dewey moisture on her fingertips, she wiped it off playfully, and sensually put her finger to her lips and then his.

Max groaned softly, then involuntarily and his self control was gone. He didn't even have time to think about the last time he was with a woman who wanted to make sure he felt special and loved and the center of her attention. He let go of the passion that was locked inside him for so long now. His head fell back to the pillow and his mouth opened slightly. Dori stroked gently a few more times helping him release all that he had been holding back. His arms just fell to his side as he let out a deep exhale. Dori covered them both with the bedsheet that had been pushed to the edge of the bed during their lovemaking and let her head rest on the pillow next to him. Their breathing quieted to normal as the aroma of sex permeated and calmed the room better than any store bought aromatherapy candle.

CHAPTER TWENTY ONE

THE AFTER GLOW

When Max woke up, Dori was lying next to him, naked and sleeping peacefully. He wanted to wake up like this every day, with his heart bursting with happiness and love. It was something he wished would be forever. Forever, he repeated to himself. That's what teenagers in love for the first time say after the first time they have sex. I want to do this every day forever. I will love you forever. Everything good was going to be a *forever* when you are young and don't know any better. Max was way past young, but he too wanted his own forever. He deserved it.

Basking in the warmth of making love with Dori, Max sat at a bistro table for two on the upper level of the Tulsi Dining room at Om Ham. It was quiet and rarely occupied, because try as they might, most Westerners and tourists in general were in a hurry to eat and the view from downstairs was good enough for them. He was happy about that.

It was well worth the extra five minutes it took to get his tea or food for the solitude and higher vantage point. He looked out at the rice fields under the waning power of the night's full moon. They surrounded the resort's east side, away from the road that led into town. Sitting still, looking out holding a steaming cup of coffee in his hands, he knew this was the life he wanted.

It was a simple life living in nature with beauty that made him feel happy to be alive to experience it. This was the life he left Los Angeles for. He was where he wanted to be and needed no further proof or inducements. He left a note on the empty pillow next to Dori that simply read - Tulsi. It was still relatively early and the dining room would be open for another few hours before changing over to lunch. Max ordered a pot of the Guru's special tea and a slice of avocado cheesecake with two forks. Lost in his happy thoughts with his tea and cheesecake placed in front him, Max felt two hands gently kneading his neck and shoulders. He looked up to see the smiling face of the Guru, his friend and teacher Ketut Arsana.

"Guru. Hello." He stood up to exchange a warm hug with his friend. "Please sit and join me. My friend Dori will be here soon."

"If she is the one responsible for the look on your face, I will be happy to join you. We are all happy for you, Max. We see you dancing around the pool and your feet seem to barely touch the ground. This is the better version of Max than the one who was upset with every noise and complained about the frozen mini croissants. I can feel something in you that I always knew was waiting to come out. I know you feel it as well. Don't lose sight of it."

Max laughed to himself at his slow moving transformation. He knew he made an ass of himself at times getting upset with the most stupid things. According to the guru, they were all stupid things. It was embarrassing now realizing how he must have appeared to all these people who only showed him love and respect. The guru tried so hard to teach him that getting upset was always unhealthy, regardless of what it was about. Lesson learned. He knew he wouldn't forget it.

The Guru sat down next to him and no sooner than he settled into his seat than a pot of tea was placed in front of him. Om Ham was his resort, built slowly brick by brick by him and his family. Fifty people each day, from sunrise to nearly ten at night, worked mixing cement made up of the volcanic ash from high up in the mountains of Kintamani and Mount Batur.

Then they would lay the bricks and tiles that filled up their flatbed trucks right to the front door of where Om Ham would be when all the work was complete. The joy of what they were all building was shining through their sweat and ash covered hands and faces. He was loved and revered and whenever he came into the dining room, his favorite items were brought to his table immediately.

"Thank you, Guru. I always remembered how you would tell me that I had a pure heart and that if I trusted it with all my decisions I would always be happy."

"That is very true and still true today," the Guru replied. The bad moments you have are easily forgiven because you have a pure heart with good intentions. So where is this woman who makes you smile like a child?"

"I hope that's me you're talking about," Dori said announcing her arrival.

Dori was behind Max when she spoke and looked directly into the hypnotizing eyes of the Guru. She was wearing a long sleeve blue linen V-neck t-shirt that hung down over her khaki yoga pants. A Balinese beach style purse depicting three topless women carrying baskets on their heads, was slung over a shoulder. The artwork was beautiful and portrayed a much earlier time in Bali.

Dori looked comfortable and at ease like she had been living here for years. Her smile was wide and alluring, and never missing an opportunity to hug a beautiful woman, the Guru was out of his seat with his arms around her before you could say Namaste. Max would have to wait.

Max knew he was in an altered state of mind and body, but when he saw an aura of white light form an angelic arch around Guru and Dori while they hugged, he was not quite sure what to make of it. He closed and opened his eyes to see if it would still be visible and it was. He felt himself changing on the inside.

He so much wanted to leave behind the pettiness and insecurities that kept him from living in a state of mindfulness and constant ease with all of life's challenges and joys. He knew it wasn't healthy to feel that he could only be at his best when there was a loving woman in his life, but that is what he believed.

He could feel joyfulness and compassion and inner peace by himself, but for him it was only for fleeting moments if he was alone. There was being happy and there was being really happy. Max wanted to be really happy and could not go on without it.

"So nice to see you again, Ms.Dori. It seems you have found what you came for," the guru said so cryptically. The Guru grabbed a nearby chair and placed it next to him and opposite Max and helped Dori into her seat. She slid her purse under the table and joined them.

"So nice to see you again as well, Guru. In the little time I've known him, Max has told me a lot about you. Will you stay and sit with us," Dori asked?

"Yes, of course. Thank you. Excuse me for just a moment. I will be right back." When he left, Dori moved into the chair next to Max. "Good Morning, my little buddha," she said as she kissed him on the lips. She reached for his hand and laced their fingers together to rest them in her lap. Their hands together had enough heat to melt ice. "Are you going to give me a bite of that cheesecake?" she asked.

Max dug into the cake with his fork and put a nice size portion up to her lips. Dori put her lips over it and pulled the rest into her mouth leaving Max with an empty fork. "Amazing. What is it?"

"Avocado cheesecake," Max answered. He put another bite on his fork and as he brought it forward to Dori's lips, she kissed him instead. Ain't love grand.

"MMMMMM. Even better." Dori was beaming with light and affection towards this new man in her life. Her questions and confusion about what to do going forward seemed gone from her mind. There are always blips in people's paths, or in this case, cracks in the sidewalks, but her inner thoughts were quiet now. She would go where her heart takes her.

The Guru returned to their table as their lips parted and placed a cup and saucer in front of Dori and poured her tea. As her cup filled, two waiters came up the steps to their table each carrying a tray of fruits and shredded coconut.

"This is from my garden, please enjoy. You must replenish your energy so you make love again. You are two old souls who find each other in Bali. Come to class Sunday morning. I see you there for a blessing afterwards."

"Thank you, Guru. We will be there," Max promised.

"Thank you for joining us and these beautiful trays," Dori added as she stood up and put her hands in the hands of the Guru. He held his warm healing hands over hers for a moment longer than expected, letting his energy flow into her. He let go and kissed her on the forehead, then whispered something into her ear. After his private comment he spoke to them as a couple.

"You are a beautiful woman. I see you together, shoulder to shoulder now. You take care of each other and love each other." The Guru turned away and was down the stairs and headed back to his ashram across the street.

"What did he whisper to you," Max asked?

"He said to come to the ashram later for a private tour. Is that where you lived?"

"I lived here for most of my stay. It was better for me with the twenty four hour reception desk and security. The ashram is pretty spartan. It's a big room with small cots and ceiling fans. It does have a more spiritual feeling to it, but having a private bathroom and the air conditioning made things a lot more comfortable for me. I guess I'm still a Westerner in some ways."

"I think that was the right move, Max. It's easy enough to walk across the street for classes and the events you've told me about. I'm with you on the pool and the A.C."

"You know, I would love to have an open window for some fresh air when there is a wind and nice breeze from the mountains. But, no one ever heard of screens around here. So it's cold AC or fresh air and mosquitoes. Maybe I should talk to Wayan about going into a new business? So, when is your private tour?"

"In a few hours. I'll find you back here after, okay?" "Sounds great, beautiful girl. I hope you like it as much as I did."

Dori reached under the table and brought her purse up to the chair next to her. She reached in and pulled out Max's journal. "I had no idea what to do with this until now, after we made love. I felt something with you, Max, and I believe you felt something with me. It was more than sex. And the sex was amazing. There should be nothing to hide for either of us. You can tell me anything and I will listen with no judgement. I want to know the real Max from virtues to flaws."

When Max opened his journal and saw his letters in their envelopes, a million thoughts raced through his mind.

"So, I guess you read them?"

"Are you kidding? Of course I did. I wasn't sure I was going to, but with three hours before my flight to Thailand and no magazines, my curiosity got the better of me."

Dori smiled warmly at Max and took his hand and held it in her lap. "It's why I changed my ticket and came here. After talking to you at the cafe for so long, and then reading these letters, it didn't add up to me. I couldn't believe you were coming here with such dark thoughts. They were goodbye letters, right?"

"In my mind, that's exactly what they were. Writing is my way of getting all my thoughts out and looking at them rationally. I was never going to mail any of them. They were for me. For my perspective on my life now and going forward in relation to what was in the past. Does that make any sense?"

"Perfect sense, Dori agreed. Writing is a very cathartic experience for me too, so I totally get it."

"Life isn't a straight line of fun and happiness. If we really live a full life, we all have moments of tragedy and hardship. It's what makes us who we are," Max added.

"Yes we do. I will say, your letters were… shall we say, expressive?" "I've been told I can be a little dramatic at times."

"You? You're kidding right," Dori said laughing. Save them, Max. These letters are what brought you into my life. I wouldn't change a thing."

It wasn't lost on Max that in just a week's time, he met two pretty amazing women. One, because of a shredded credit card, and the other because of lost letters. How crazy is that? Max leaned in and kissed his sweetheart.

"I'm glad you found them, but I have an idea. There are monthly cacao ceremonies at all the hotels and even at the Pyramids of Chi. There is a Master Cacao barista of sorts and a big fire pit, and people gather around the fire to burn away the past and celebrate new beginnings with a ceremonial drink. Will you do that with me? I don't need them anymore."

"You bet. We especially have to get rid of that Laurie girl. I'm sorry she hurt you so deeply, Max." She kissed Max and put the letters back in her purse for safe keeping.

"It's all right. I'm over the hurt part, and it was the beginning of a big change for me. It started my spiritual practice and led me here, to Bali, and eventually, to you. I couldn't be happier, Dori."

"Me too. I hope you live here for many years if that's what you want. Who knows, right? Maybe I will be here with you and we can invite all of our friends every now and then for a big party. What do you think?"

"It sounds great to me. Enough of this mushy stuff. You go do your ashram thing. Just don't let the guru hug you too tight."

"Max, before I go, I want to say something now that we have made love for the first time. Dori didn't wait for him to interrupt her. "As close as we've become and the openness in our lovemaking, I can still feel that when emotions get really close, a little wall starts to go up. I don't want that wall to get any bigger. I want it to come down."
"Dori…

"Let me finish. Please. I feel like we're reaching a point where we can either go forward, or stop with what we have. I understand the pain you've gone through. I feel like I love you and I guess what I'm really wanting to say here is- don't be afraid of that love".

"Dori, I'm not. I love you and I hope you know that." Dori put her hands on his shoulders and looked into his eyes. "I do know that. I just don't want you to be afraid to love me without hesitation. Without wondering if what you say or do will cause me to run. It won't. You got that, my little buddha?"

Max put his arms around her and kissed her. "I got it." Dori got up from her chair and Max got up as well. "Thank you for listening. I hope I wasn't out of line. Anyway, dear Max, I'm going to my room and take a little nap before I go to the ashram for my tour."

"Have a great time. I'm going for a swim and will do an afternoon yoga class. If I'm not here when you get back, I'll be joining the kirtan class at Sayuri. It starts at 6:00. You can join me there for a snack after or we'll find each other here. How's that?" Dori wrapped her arms around him for a long, hug.

"This has been quite a few days," she replied. It seems like an eternity. In a good way, she added with her sweet sexy laugh. "I have some things to share with you as well, if we're going to make something of this."

"What? There's more? You can't just walk away now." Max was eager to learn more about this new woman in his life and he hoped there would be many more days of sharing about their lives and making love in Bali.

"Soon, dear Max." With another gentle kiss to his lips, she left their embrace and walked towards her room for her nap. She walked off happy she spilled the beans about finding his journal, and even happier that this new man in her life was ready to share everything about himself.

Max was feeling very lucky and blessed. He knew he sabotaged himself many times before when having a truly loving relationship for the long haul meant being for more generous in terms of revealing who he was at his core, and being honest about his insecurities. At least, until now.

Dori has now seen him with his walls down and emotions exposed, and she was still here. Dori felt the same. She was relieved her talk with Max went so well and it confirmed what she thought about him all along. She was not a woman who fell for the edgy, aloof men who thought too much of themselves. Not any more. Self confidence was one thing, but an overloaded ego was not for her. The less the ego, the more the man she learned.

He sat back down to polish off the few bites of cheesecake left on their plate. The warmth and love from Dori's hug lingered and he sat quietly, gazing contentedly out into the rice fields.

CHAPTER TWENTY TWO

CEREMONIES OF LIFE

If it wasn't for the sound of kids splashing in the pool, Max might have slept until morning. He had fallen asleep on one of the double wide chaise lounge chairs parked under a big umbrella. The sun was now mostly orange as it began its final descent behind the yoga room on the fourth floor. He walked up the stairs quickly to catch the last of the sunset and the magical views from the roof. It was a nightly scene worth catching.

White Heron's would nose dive into the water filled trenches for a quick dinner while workers carried their day's work out of the rice paddies. They looked like the Sherpas of Nepal hauling hikers' supplies going up Mount Everest, but here, they were working to feed their families.

They would load huge bales of rice over their shoulders to take home for the final steps of the harvest that would be sold at local markets and placed on their kitchen tables.

He often fell asleep on one of the wicker recliners put there for that very reason. It never got old. When he finally made it to his room, he saw a card resting against his door. It had flowers and butterflies along the border and his name in bold blue Sharpie in the center. He opened it quickly.

MAX
I didn't see you at the pool, and there

was no answer when I knocked on your door.
I had the most wonderful time at the ashram
with the guru. I met some of his family at
his healing room and we shared tea and fruit.
He gave me a blessing and did a short hands
on healing. I can't do anything but sleep
right now. I love this place.

Hugs and Kisses

Dori
XOXOXOXO

P.S
Your friend Wayan texted me and is picking
me up at 7:00 A.M to see the village healer
Made' you told me so many stories about.
So many new experiences. I will text you
when my session is over. See you soon.

Max felt a bit dejected at not getting to spend the night with
Dori, but he was happy that she would meet his friend and get an
unforgettable insight into her life- past, present and future. He
put the note on his bed and went back to the pool for a much
needed swim. He missed the last yoga class at the ashram, and
the kirtan at Sayuri; but, he felt great and his mind was at ease.
There was really no missing anything in Bali. You miss a class on
Tuesday and there is another on Wednesday. Wash, rinse, repeat.
A swim under the stars would be a great end to the evening. And
even better, he has a woman in his life who cares about him. Life
is good.

CHAPTER TWENTY THREE

DORI'S READING

Wayan's van pulled up to the beautiful gardens of Made's home. He parked under a sign that said Ubad Ubud, which means Ubud medicine man. The home was surrounded by huge Banyan trees and plenty of coconut palms and it took only a few steps onto the property to feel the sense of calm that filled the air for all who entered. Wayan was a long time friend and always had Made's blessing to bring guests he felt would appreciate and respect his work.

He would explain to everyone he brought that Made' was the village healer and his gift of herbal remedies and fortune telling were mostly reserved for the Balinese people who lived in his neighborhood. Wayan gave Dori a brief explanation as he escorted her to the meditation waiting area, and then retreated to his van to wait until her session was over.

Made' came out of his healing room and temple wearing a white sarong and white linen pullover shirt that was open to just above his stomach. He was wearing his ceremonial attire and his body was adorned with heavy beads that hung low around his neck. He was in all white, right up to the udon resting neatly on top of his wavy black hair.

No matter what he was wearing, the first thing anyone would notice about him was his huge smile. Made' was tall and he had what his friends would call a happy belly. His aura was always clear and peaceful. He would look at you and smile and hold out his hand, and you would feel safe. His presence was that strong.

Made''s wife, Dewi, which means goddess, was an incredible cook and taught Balinese cooking classes to tourist groups. She always had samples waiting for the guests that were fresh from the student's skillets in her kitchen. She would pass out bottled water and collect the donation to sit with her husband. The donation was $300,000 IDR which on most days, would equal just under twenty one dollars American. It was more than fair, especially considering an hour with such a man in such a peaceful setting as this, would easily cost two hundred dollars American in Los Angeles. It wasn't unusual for the friends of those getting a reading from Made' to sign up for cooking classes. It was a win for everyone.

Made' walked over to Dori with an extended hand just as his wife covered Dori's clothing with a ceremonial sarong that wrapped around her to prepare for being inside the temple. "Welcome to my home, Ms, Dori. I'm so happy to meet you. Did you prepare your most important three questions?"

"Thank you, Made'. Yes, I did. I'm ready. Max told me so much about you and his readings with you. Thank you for seeing me today."

"After my first meeting with Max, I called him my brother. He has a special gift in his heart, and any friend of his is welcome to my home any time. Leave your shoes at the temple door and come inside."

Dori followed him as he walked up the three stone steps into his temple. Inside, the room was filled with stone statues of Shiva, Hanoman, and Ganesha as well as a small fountain that held his holy water. Long sandalwood sticks of incense burned from all four corners. A far cry from the environment at the ten dollar psychic reading booth on the corner of Sunset and Fairfax in Hollywood.

Made' was always friendly to all who entered his home, but when it was time for his sessions, and before each spiritual reading, he liked to stay in a state of meditation and quiet. He would sit in the Eastern corner of his temple, douse himself with a few drops of holy water from his well, and say a few prayers. Then, it was time to begin.

Dori sat down in lotus pose and took three deep breaths as instructed. While she did that, Made' sprinkled holy water from his well over her head and splashed a few drops on her face. His eyes closed and he chanted a slow AUM sound for a minute, said a prayer and took Dori's hands in his. He then took a small leather pouch of loose beads and shook them before spilling them onto the floor. They spread out in clusters and a few danced off to one side or the other. Made' looked at them and then asked Dori, "what is your first question?"

Meanwhile, while Dori was with Made', Max used his time to take a quick swim and do fifteen minutes of the breathing techniques he learned from his time at the ashram. Arta introduced Balinese Pranayama to him and it became a regular part of his practice. They were a series of different arm positions while doing rapid breathing followed by holding the breath. Whenever he would complete an intense set like this, his mind was clear and his body was rested. He could feel that at these moments, he had the answers to any of his questions.

Wayan sent him a text while Dori was getting her reading revealing he would be dropping Dori at Sayuri Healing Foods around 11:00 and that she would like for him to meet her there if he could.

Max was happy to oblige. He enjoyed the shuttle rides into town for any number of reasons, but mostly because they presented an opportunity to meet new guests from all over the world who happened to choose Om Ham as their hotel. He loved to share some of his favorite places and help people new to Bali make sense of the streets and alleyways where one could find so many of the local treasures.

Sometimes the front desk manager would introduce him as the Mayor of Om Ham if the group was obviously American. Max didn't mind at all. His old days as an Uber driver in Los Angeles were still with him in some ways.

The shuttle finally slowed to a stop in the dirt driveway next to the restaurant. He was barely out of the van when he saw Dori sitting on a wooden bench next to the front door. She was wearing khaki colored shorts and a tie dye t-shirt with a peace sign in the center. The shuttle driver was struck by her beauty and gave Max a big smile of approval as he stepped out to meet her. He was young and still learning English, but enjoyed sharing aspects of what social life is like for him and his friends.

There are so many misconceptions about sex in Bali and Max enjoyed learning about them. The Balinese millennials were not shy about sex, only modest about it in public. They had their fair share of playboys and scoundrels just as anywhere, but at a certain age, the men in the families had to grow up and take responsibility, and get married. If they were not married by the age of thirty five, they had to leave the family home. But they cheered on love for everyone.

Sometimes too much for Max, as he remembered more than a few times he had to get off a scooter taxi because the driver wanted to take him to see a Balinese woman friend who was close by… which was short for come have some sexual pleasure that was left up to the people involved. It wasn't a morality thing, he just didn't feel comfortable on the back of a sketchy looking scooter driver asking him if he wanted to go "Boom Boom, meet fine young woman."

"Hi Dori, Max beamed with excitement. How was your reading?"

"I'm still hearing his words in my head. It was incredible, actually. He told me things from my past and about people in my life. I had goosebumps and a few tears. I'll never forget it. Thank you, Max. Let's get a table and I'll tell you all about it. I'm really hungry now."

They walked in together, with Dori's hand around Max's waist. She was noticeably fond of him and had no problem showing it. Max didn't mind either. It had been too long to remember since a woman he cared about treated him in such an affectionate way. A way that said to everyone else around, this guy's with me. They found a quiet table for two in the back and Max was eager to hear the details from Dori's session.

"Did he throw the beads from his pouch," he asked?

"That was crazy. I don't know how he interpreted a few beads in one corner and a few others scattered on the floor. But he looked at them for a minute and then as if he saw my life unfold in front of him, he told me about my sister who was never born. There was a miscarriage. My mom didn't even tell me about it for a really long time. Then he told me she was born soon afterwards to a different mother and a loving home. That's when the goosebumps and tears came."

"Damn. That is crazy. He did that with me. There were three beads in one pile and the rest scattered around in front of him. He looked at the three beads together and then looked at me and said, "You are the eldest of three boys, yes?" I just nodded and then he looked at me so intensely and said, "I'm sorry. Your mom passed recently. Is that right?"

"I said yes, and then I had tears." He just looked at me and said, "Your mom is here now, right behind you. She says for you to get out of your house more." Then he just took my hand and told me a few things, did some breathing with me and sprinkled a little holy water on me and that was it. When my time was over, he just gave me a big hug and told me I was a brother to him and I could ask him for anything but money. The Balinese people can be very direct like that. It's kind of funny and sweet. And it's the moments like these that keep me wanting to come back."

"You know, it's kind of interesting now to be with you here relating to something else he told me." "What was that," Dori asked?

"Well, when I told him I was going back to California but only to pack up a few things and come back here to live, he told me to go slow. He said there is a woman in America for me but that it could take a year or longer to meet her."

Dori's eyes opened wide wanting to know more. "That's pretty specific. What did you say?"

"I told him I love Bali too much to wait a year or longer and that if there was a woman I was supposed to meet, I would just have to meet her here." "Or maybe on an airplane here?" Dori added mischievously.

With menus in hand and comfortable in their seats, Max pointed to a few of his favorites, like the vegan Reuben on dark rye, and the dragon fruit bowl with crunchy spirulina as a topping.

"My God, Max. How do I choose. I could eat everything on this menu. Those cakes and pies at the register, these smoothie bowls. I don't even know where to start." Max offered a compromise of sorts. "How about lunch first, then desert and maybe we take a desert or two home with us?"

Dori agreed. "I like the way you think." She quickly pointed to the vegan Reuben sandwich and Max ordered the grilled tempeh panini with sweet potato fries to get things underway. The food was so good it was not on their plates for long, and the conversation was easy as they got deeper into learning about each other in terms of dreams and desires.

It wasn't long before the wait staff cleared their table and brought out their after lunch coffee and organic pumpkin pie. Dori wasn't a coffee drinker and opted for something she had never seen on a menu before, the charcoal tea latte'. Max was still curious about Dori's reading, and wondered if he was mentioned in any way, like maybe as a new man in her life. One thing he knew for sure, Made' would not share what was part of their private session.

"So what else did Made' tell you," he asked with a bit of a wink in his eye. Am I being nosy?"

"Not at all. He told me two things that meant a lot to me. First, he told me it was good I came to Bali to find you. And before you let that go to your head and get any idea of things, next, he told me my path was to go on with my yoga program in Thailand and to stay true to my plans. He said they were right for me at this time."

"So that's good, right?" I mean, *I'm* glad you came to Bali to find me. And I'm glad I didn't wait until I met someone and wondered if she was the one he was talking about. I don't like it when certain seeds get planted in your mind and you're always wondering, "is this the person from the reading, is this the job I was supposed to take, etc. You know what I mean?"

"I sure do, Dori answered. It seems like we both have something new to process and make a decision about." "I'm good with the way things are going," Max said confidently. "Are you?"

"Yes. I'm really happy to be here with you Max. And I even feel like I could stay and do yoga here just as easily as in Thailand. But Thailand is only a few weeks and I can always come back here before going home if things go in that direction. But there were some other things Made' shared with me, and I think it's important for me- maybe even for us, to let those things play out. I'm going to go to Thailand for my yoga training. It's something I have been planning for over a year and I want to do it."

"I think that's an awesome plan," Max said with a smile. Let's walk around town and burn some calories, unless you want to burn them in a more creative environment."

"A walk sounds just fine, my little Romeo. Let's see what you have left once the sun goes down."

Max took her hand laughing and led her out the door and down Hanoman street. He didn't have a reply and learned long ago that no reply was much better received than a stupid one. They walked the narrow streets of Ubud Center stopping in clothing stores, gift shops and checking menus at whatever looked like a possibility for another time. He was walking lightly, worry free and a million miles away from wondering what to do with the rest of his life. His thoughts were on the present, the here and now. He didn't want to lose sight of that.

Fun conquered time, and when they missed the last shuttle, Max hailed two scooter taxis. One for him, one for Dori. This is an experience that is equal to or better than many of the tourist attractions in his opinion. In fact, Max thought it should be listed under the ten best things to do while in Bali.

He quietly told each driver their destination and they sped off, each gripping the waist of their driver as they weaved in and out of traffic, dodged on coming cars and trucks and held on for dear life. Max was a bit envious of the young man driving Dori, as she wrapped her arms around the man's waist and held on tight. He would have to learn how to drive a scooter. The sooner the better.

Night had come faster than expected and the day's events had Dori's eyes closed and her head resting on Max's shoulder as they were driven back to Om Ham by one of the hotel's drivers. Max sat with his eyes closed, but awake, his left hand interlocked with Dori's right. He was at peace, uplifted from their day of great food, laughter, rides on scooter taxis and a quick trip to the famous Campuhan Ridge Walk and incredible Antapan Waterfall.

They did most of the five mile hike through rice fields, over the sacred Campuhan River Bridge, and spent a few minutes at the majestic Pura Gunung Lebah Temple. It's a breathtaking walk, and offers the clarity of life that comes from being in a pristine outback of indescribable beauty far removed from the hotel and restaurant lined streets of central Ubud. Dori's eyes opened as their van pulled into the parking area of Om Ham. Max helped her out and they walked to their rooms happily together with a day of fun and adventure behind them and the comfort of a budding relationship ahead of them. A night made for deep sleep and sweet dreams.

The succeeding days evolved into nights as smoothly as the sun drops into the ocean and they passed as quickly as a shooting star through the midnight sky. The Full Moon Ceremony at the Ashram, the nights of kirtan at the Yoga Barn, and the side trips into villages off the beaten path all made for memories neither Dori or Max would soon forget. If anything, the time was going by too quickly for Max, as he knew Dori was soon leaving for Thailand.

Dori never did tell him about the more personal revelations she received from Made' during her reading, and there was also the time she spent with the Guru after the full moon ceremony in his private room. Max was never one to pry and even though he didn't know Dori for long, he knew her enough to trust her with whatever she wanted to share or not share. Anyway, he knew enough to know it was not up to him.

They each shared a lot of their lives from growing up in their hometowns to college and working in the world and all that got them to this point in life. Everyone has things they keep to themselves. At least until they feel safe enough and the time is right. Bali is a place where hearts and minds open to their fullest. Fears dissolve into trust with the willingness to let go of the past and just acknowledge it for what it is. For what it was. What got you to where you are now.

CHAPTER TWENTY FOUR

GOOD-BYE FOR NOW

Max woke up alone in his bed. The pillow and sheets to his left were ruffled but empty. As his eyes opened wider, he noticed a neatly folded card with his name written across the front. It was propped up against a glass of water holding a beautiful yellow rose.

He reached over to grab the note, deciding it might be better to read while still in bed with Dori's pheromones still saturating the bedsheets. The scent of her sex was his aphrodisiac of choice as well as what instilled a level of calm inside him he had not experienced since his days of daily yoga and massage at the ashram. He took a deep breath in through his nose and let it out slowly through his mouth. Letting go of that chi energy as he was taught. He did that two more times and then to no one in particular he said, " alright, let's see what we got here".

> Dear Max
> First, I want to say I am sorry for slipping
> out of your room without waking you. I knew
> if I did, I would want to make love to you
> again and feel your warm hands and sweet
> kisses all over me. MMMMMMM. Thank you dear
> Max for sharing so much of yourself these
> last days together. I loved seeing you in

yoga and kirtan singing and chanting and
hearing about your dreams to lead your own
group and have spiritual talks open for
anyone who wants to come. You have a gift to
make people feel safe and comfortable to
share any problems they might be facing. You
will make a wonderful spiritual coach and
teacher and I hope you follow your heart and
stay true to all you want for yourself. Now
here's the hard part. I've been in remission
for two years and had forgotten all about
being sick. I started feeling things in my
body and both Made' and the Guru confirmed
my suspicions. My cancer may be coming back.
I have many options and am hopeful it will go
away for good once I get back to my doctor in
Los Angeles. I need this time to myself to
sort it all out, and I will call/email soon
after my classes in Thailand. Our days and
nights together fill my heart and there are
very few minutes in the day that I don't
think of you and all we shared. I love you.
Be good to yourself. Follow your heart always
and know we will be together soon.
     Love,
     DORI
     XO

All the deep breaths he could take were not enough for the news he just read. How could this be, he wondered? He felt like his best life just started. With tears in his eyes, he made his morning coffee and brought it and the glass of water with the rose inside still in bloom outside to one of the tables at the pool. He sat, reading the note over and over between sips of coffee until he realized that reading it over and over again would not change the words.

He finally put it aside. He dropped himself into the deep end of the pool, hanging onto the ledge staring out into the rice fields. The soothing warm water and early morning sun were all that stood between him and doing something really stupid, like getting on the next flight to Bangkok. He stayed in place, gently moving his legs in the water holding tight to the step bars at his end of the pool. He was wiping water from his eyes when he saw the worn sandals and dark skinned feet of the guru stop in front of him.

"Come later to my home," the guru said in his gentle but commanding tone that offered no opportunity to resist. We will have tea. He reached down and placed his hand on Max's head and left it there for a moment. Long enough to pass his blessings and healing energy to his friend. Max didn't need to say anything, and that was a good thing, because words were not coming out of his mouth just yet. Tea? Is he kidding? He wanted something much stronger.

He dressed slowly, completely disinterested in his appearance. He felt blindsided. How could the most wonderful night he had in many years become the worst morning he could imagine just a few hours later? Remission. This amazing woman who in the span of seven days changed his outlook on life through her love and total incredibleness, was in remission and out the door asking for time to deal with the changes in her life. Seven days Max thought. Then he laughed because he was out of tears. He laughed because that was all he had at the moment. He had seven *days* of heaven with a woman who filled his heart and justified his constant hopefulness and belief that everything always works out.

Max took the shuttle into town. His thoughts were much like the hamster in his wheel, starting and ending in the same place. He had enough death in his life so it only made sense that the shuttle was barely moving, stuck behind a funeral procession. It was of no consequence to him. Actually, he was thankful for it. He was not ready to talk to anyone. The feelings he had now, reminded him of how he felt before his first trip to Bali.

In a span of six months, his dog died in his arms, the woman he loved said she loved someone else, his best friend for all his life died on his birthday, and his mother died a few months after that. When he tried to talk to his doctor about all of this during his annual physical, the only thing the doctor said was, " I'm sorry to hear that. It sounds like a Greek tragedy. Do you need anything to help you sleep?" Only if it kept me asleep, he joked to himself.

The shuttle finally stopped at Bodyworks. Before going in, Max walked a few blocks down the street to get some cookies and bread for the guru and his family. Whenever he went to see him, he always brought treats without being asked. This time wasn't any different, except that he was being summoned instead of showing up on his own to say hi and chat.

He knew the guru was just trying to keep him busy with a task and help him tap into what inside him will get him through this time. Max walked past the office and meditation area boxes in hand. The guru was sitting by the Koi pond and had a pot of tea and two cups at his table.

"Hello Max. Come sit down."

Max put the snacks on the table and sat down. "Hi Guru. I know you know what's going on. Dori left me a note that she saw you a few days ago at the ashram. Is she going to be okay?"

"I believe she will, Max. I made her a very powerful root tea and herbal rub and I think it will stop her symptoms before they turn into the cancer that was there before."

"She went to Thailand to do her yoga training. Is that good," he asked?

"Yes. She is very strong and the temple she will be at for her training is one of the best. It will keep her mind clear and her body healthy. She is more worried about you, than herself. She asked me to tell you to stay on your course. Do your yoga, sing with your friends and start your own kirtan group. She said if you do that, you will be happy and she will be happy for you."

"I love her guru. I came back to Bali because I felt like I lost my purpose these last two years back in the states. I figured I would just be here and eat and play until the end, as long as that would be. Then I met Dori, and all I wanted was to see what kind of life we could make together. Here or anywhere."

"She told me the same. Now go, get a massage, drink your tea. The staff at Om Ham will bring you tea throughout the day for the next week. I want you to fast starting tonight for a few days. Then you will come to the ashram for a healing session. This is life, Max. We all come and go, so each day must be our best. There is no sad thing in life if we understand how to look at it. That is why you see the same processions in the streets of Ubud for a funeral or a wedding."

Max wiped away a few tears with his sleeve. He hugged the guru goodbye, then made his way out to Hanoman street. He felt better and he knew that this was maybe his last shot at putting all his energy into doing what he had been dreaming about for the last few years. He was loved and ready to do the work to love himself and feel the gratitude for the life he has every single day he is blessed with it.

CHAPTER TWENTY FIVE

DECISIONS

Dori sat on a bench outside the main entrance for the Ngurah Rai International Airport in Denpasar. Her flight was in three hours and she was not quite ready to go inside and go through the ticketing and gate areas. That was too official. She checked her watch and did the math. Two P.M in Bali means ten P.M the previous day in Los Angeles. This was a perfect time to call Allie.

She needed the words of wisdom from her dear friend now more than ever. She trusted Made' and the guru, but Allie knew her from the inside out and better than any medicine man in a foreign land. No offense Made' she uttered to no one in particular. Dori Dialed and waited as the phone rang on the other end eight thousand miles away.

"Dori, finally, I was getting worried about you. Did you find Max? Are you good? Are you still going to do your yoga in Thailand?"

"Hi Allie. Yes, I found Max and well, it's like we had a year of life in a week. I'm sorry for not being in touch, but it's been a whirlwind. I just left his bed a few hours ago and now I'm at the airport. I don't know what to do." As she spoke those last few words, her voice tailed off into an emotional whisper.

"Honey, tell me. What is it? Did he hurt you? Was he mean to you? I'll fly there right now and twist his little head off right out from under those prayer beads of his."

Dori laughed that laugh of relief a person feels when they know they are safe and talking with their best friend. "Ohhh Allie. I do wish you were here right now. And no. Max did not hurt me. He is a sweet, kind man and I fell in love with him this week. It's something else. I'm actually at the airport. My flight to Thailand is in three hours but I don't want to go."

"What *do you* want," Allie asked? "I want to stay here with Max. It's only been a little over a week but I feel like I've known him all my life. I did the moment we met on the plane."

Dori and Allie talked for another hour, and with no prodding at all, she was booking the next flight to Denpasar and Dori was calling Wayan to see if he was near-by. She needed that old familiar voice of reason from her best friend to ask her simply and directly, "what the fuck are you doing?"

Allie had the mouth of a drunken sailor and the looks of a runway model. When Dori told her about her remission, Allie had a simple and predictable reaction if you knew her for more than a week. "Screw that," she said. Her reasoning was simple. You don't fly ten thousand miles and take a side trip through some yoga based third world country to chase after a hippie with crystal bracelets only to give it all up over some bullshit remission. "I'll see you in two days or however long these fucking flights take," she added.

"Allie, wait. Let me see how I feel. I don't want you to come all this way for me to end up on a flight back to Los Angeles in who knows how long. If I really get back to Los Angeles, I'd be much happier and better off if you were there waiting for me. I'll call you in a couple of days, okay?"

"Okay. A couple is two. If I don't hear from you in two days, I'm coming out."

Dori couldn't reply fast enough. Allie hung up and for all she knew, her bff was checking flights.

It was already heavy duty rush hour traffic and it would be a two hour drive back to Ubud and Om Ham. That was too much to deal with after such an emotional day, so when Wayan arrived at the airport, Dori asked him to take her somewhere nice for the night.

Maya Sanur was a great choice. Sanur is a small beach town. It was near the airport and similar to Manhattan Beach in Southern California. Dori loved seeing all the small shops, boutiques and roadside restaurants they passed along the way. She hadn't been to the beach yet in Bali and she felt good to have a little space from everything and someplace new to explore. Wayan helped her into the hotel lobby with her bags, and told her as always, call when you need anything.

Dori looked around and was taken in by the incredible art and sculptures that filled the spacious lobby. This was a luxurious beachfront hotel and a much different vibe than the nice, but economical and spiritually centered Om Ham. In less than a minute, there was a beautiful young Balinese woman holding a tray in front of her, offering a choice of drinks, chocolates and fresh fruit while she waited for the registration desk to be free.

"Good evening Ms. Dori, the registration clerk said as she looked at Dori's passport. Welcome to Maya Sanur. How long will you be with us?" "Two nights, maybe three. Can I tell you later?"

"Of course, the clerk said. Putu will be here in just a moment to take your bags and lead you to your room. I put you upstairs with a private balcony facing the ocean. Dinner is available until nine and the beachfront grill is open until eleven. Please enjoy your stay." "Thank you. That sounds wonderful."

Dori sat down with her chocolates and welcome drink and let out a long sigh. It had been a long and emotional day. Writing the note to Max took a lot out of her and now, here she was, still in Bali wondering what her next days would bring. She was glad she didn't return to Om Ham. She felt bad to keep Max in the dark for right now, but she needed a little time to herself and a beachfront hotel in the lap of luxury seemed like a good move.

Meanwhile in Ubud, Max felt like all the stress and worry had been massaged out of him. When he was dressed, he left a generous tip on the table. The guru did a little extra work on him before his massage that probably left a mark, but he knew he needed it. He walked down the steep stairway to the garden and the guru was waiting for him with a pot of tea and some ginger spiced cookies.

"You look much better. How is my handsome friend?"

"I'm good. It still feels weird that Dori would leave without seeing me, but it's okay. I feel like going to Thailand to find her and tell her we can be together no matter what the problem is. Is that stupid?"

"Do what your heart tells you, Max. For now, get a good sleep and see how you feel in the morning. I gave you some deep work."

"I know. I feel it already. I'm going to sit here until I can walk without crashing into a wall."

The guru gave Max a hug and tapped on his heart. "Whatever you do from here, is good." The guru then went back upstairs to his healing room leaving Max to sit still in the garden watching the Koi fish.

While Max was letting the guru's deep body work settle into his body and mind, Dori was waking up in her new surroundings feeling relieved and hungry. She opened the curtains to a breathtaking view of the Indian Ocean. The water was a beautiful teal blue and was quiet to start the day. Children were already playing in the water and in the distance, local fishermen in their traditional wooden outrigger canoes, called *jukungs,* as well as small motor boats, puttered out to sea hoping to bring home breakfast and lunch.

It was peaceful to see how life in small villages was still the same in many ways. Small white capped waves crashed gently to the shore stopping just short of the cushioned lounge chairs being cleaned and made ready for another day of sunbathers and swimmers. Life is slow. You don't rush Bali.

Dori made her way to the breakfast area, getting pulled closer and closer by the sights and aromas of more than a dozen food stations each manned by its own chef. The head chef stood at the ready, serving tools in hand wearing his starched white chef's jacket and hat beckoning the early risers to the morning buffet. The hot choices ranged from chicken and pork and a wide of array of porridges, to whatever egg dish you could imagine. There was a wide variety of hot breads coming right out of the ovens including croissants, rolls, dark and white breads, and even sourdough made San Francisco style.

The cold choices were equally incredible and included ham, turkey, and other deli slices, along with fruits, salads, yogurts, juices and deserts. One could easily spend a morning eating to exhaustion. Dori grabbed a plate of eggs and fruit to get started, walking to a table with an ocean view. Her phone chimed with the news of a What's App text message. It was Allie. She was like a Jewish grandmother and was checking in to make sure all was well and to repeat that she was still ready to be on her way in a moment's notice.

Good friends are hard to find, and Dori was grateful to have her childhood friend in her life. Since her father died and being an only child, a little mothering now and then felt good. Her energy was high again and she felt good enough to go right back to the buffet. Time for some Balinese chicken, fresh hot sourdough bread and a long conversation with her girl back home.

Back at Om Ham, Max was up early sitting at the Tulsi dining room working out his next move. "More coffee, Mr. Max," Koming asked?

"To go cup, please Koming. I am off to the airport to find Ms. Dori and bring her back here." "Yes, Mr. Max. Good luck to find Ms. Dori. She is very nice. We are all happy she stays here. Reception called to tell you Mr. Wayan is at the entrance waiting for you."

"Thank you, Koming." With a quick bow to Koming, Max grabbed his coffee and walked to the carport. The sliding back doors to Wayan's van were open and waiting for him. His energy was high and his purpose was set. He was not going to let this woman walk out of his life. Whatever the circumstances are, they will deal with it together.

"Good morning, Wayan. Airport please. I'm going to see if I can get a ticket to Bangkok and find Ms. Dori at her yoga retreat."

"Good morning, Mr. Max. I'm sorry, but you don't have to go to Thailand to find Ms. Dori." "What do you mean? I thought you took her to the airport yesterday. She left me a note about Thailand."

"I did take her, Mr. Max. She called me two hours later to come get her. She said she wanted to stay. I took her to the Maya Sanur Hotel on the beach."

"Shit! Wayan. Sorry for the language. Are you kidding me? What happened?" "No Mr. Max. Not kidding. Did I do something wrong for you?"

"No. Not at all. I'm just surprised. I don't know what's going on, Did she say anything to you?"

"She called and said she didn't want to go to Thailand and to take her somewhere nice. She said she wants to be here in Bali with you. You like to go there now?"

"I don't know. I would like to, but maybe it's better for me to wait for her to call. At least for today. At least I know she is still here. What do you think?"

"I think very good idea, Mr. Max. Everything will happen as it should. That's what my wife always tells me when I worry about my business."

"You have a smart wife, Wayan. Maybe if I'm smart, I will have a wife." "You will, Mr. Max," Wayan assured.

Max paid Wayan for his drive time and added a little extra for his words of wisdom. What he said was true for all people everywhere. Everything will happen as it should. Max had a lot of nervous energy to unload and decided to take a walk to his favorite local juice bar, Bali Pure, and just hang out there and be a local. It was a twenty to thirty minute walk from Om Ham and marked the halfway spot between Om Ham and Ubud town center. Walking was a nice change of pace. It provided an opportunity to see much more of the land and people when not buzzing by at thirty MPH on a scooter taxi. It also made it much easier to find the small walkway off the main road that led to the well hidden White Heron Bird Sanctuary which was about half way to his destination.

Max checked out the beautiful white birds, taking a few photos with his phone while enjoying a cool drink. He pushed forward and still made it to Bali Pure in under an hour. The mid-day sun was brutal. There was not a cloud in the sky which was unusual for this time of year. It was deep into the rainy season so Max could only wonder, what gives? By the time he sat down at one of the tables at Bali Pure, he needed a napkin to wipe the sweat from his face.

There were a few people hanging out with coconuts and juice drinks and for such a small place, Bali Pure was lively and always a fun destination and one that he always pointed out to hotel guests when they were all on the shuttle together into town. The owner, Stephan, who came to know Max over the past year, was in his fifties, a tall, tan and friendly expat from Germany.

He was carrying a tray of drinks to two women sitting at the next table and he was happy to see Max, who had become a friend. They shared lively conversations and he always made sure Max got the best bananas and mangos to take back to his room.

"You look hot, Stephan said." "I hope you don't mean that in a sexual way, Stephan," Max replied with his best serious voice.
The two women broke out laughing and eventually Stephan understood the joke and offered a smile. Max was great at deadpan humor; at least when the cameras weren't rolling. If he was that good when they were, he would have had a different career.

Not bad, Max thought to himself. It was funny enough to get a German to smile. Stephan brought him a fresh beet and apple juice with ginger and sat down to join his friend.

"How are you, Max? I haven't seen you in a while."

I'm good. A beautiful woman I met on the flight here came to visit me and we've been together for almost two weeks. I'm in love, Stephan."

"Congratulations, Max. I'm very happy for you. I hope you will bring her here. No charge for your drink today, to celebrate your good news."

"Thank you, Stephan. Is it too late to change my order?" "You're funny today, Max. I'll throw in a refill and some green bananas. How's that?"

Max hung out and talked with Stephan in between customers. Stephan moved to Bali from Germany ten years ago and opened his first organic juice bar. He opened a second place on one of the busy streets in Ubud Center, Monkey Forest Road. He was a wise and friendly man and shared some of his secrets for living a good life in Bali. Number one, according to him, if you didn't want to always be a tourist, was to marry a Balinese woman. He did and has two children.

He said that is the only way to be truly accepted, because it immerses you in their culture. Otherwise, you are always a tourist, no matter how long you stay. Max understood, but if he was going to be lucky enough to marry someone, it was not going to be a Balinese woman. It was going to be Dori Kominski, the woman on flight 2806 from Los Angeles to Hong Hong.

CHAPTER TWENTY SIX

REUNION AT THE BEACH

Learning to be patient paid off in spades as they say. Max was worn out by his walk to Bali Pure and his long chat with Stephan left him ready for quiet time. By the time he made it back to Om Ham, he was too tired to think about anything, so he settled for a long, hot shower and went to bed. He woke up to a text from Dori inviting him to come to the hotel. It was short and sweet. "I'm at Maya Sanur. Join me."

He remembered the long curved pathway to the hotel lobby the moment Wayan dropped him off. He was here on his very first trip to Bali and after ten days in Ubud, he spent the last two days at the beach. He was not the only one who ended his Bali trip with an escape from the rush and traffic of the city. The pool was filled with people from New York and Los Angeles, and you could hear conversations about the Yankees and the Dodgers as well as the occasional political shouting match about the candidates Hilary and Donald.

He was so happy to escape the constant drone of political arguments everywhere in the states, that he almost forgot there was an upcoming election. That happiness could only last so long he realized. Here he was, ten thousand miles away in a gorgeous swimming pool facing the Indian ocean, and there were enough Americans to almost ruin it with their constant yelling back and forth at each other about the evils of each candidate.

Max accepted the reality that enough Americans in any one place can ruin just about anything and just looked down at the sparking blue water hoping to drown out the voices. Fortunately, a beer drinking Aussie couple came up to him as if they were reading his mind. They made an eye roll in the direction of the loud mouths, and offered him a beer. "Join us for a beer, mate," they said together in that delightful Aussie accent. We're partying. "Twenty years married to this gorgeous little birdie," the husband shouted to everyone. The people at the pool stopped for a moment and gave the couple a hearty applause and loud cheer. Well deserved, Max thought.

The lady at the registration desk, Shanti, wouldn't give him the room number, but offered to ring Dori's room and tell her she had a guest. Max settled for that and waited on a beautiful rattan lounge chair. One of the hostesses brought him a welcome tray of drinks and chocolates and he sat back with his treats wondering what to say, wondering if he should be happy or angry that he wasn't told about this detour. Mercifully, his monkey mind was interrupted by the beautiful woman he was falling in love with.

"Hey stranger. Are you stalking me?"

As always, from the very first moment he saw her walking down the aisle on their flight to Hong Kong, Dori was a vision of beauty to his eyes.

"Yes I am. And I will be from this day forward. You got a problem with that," Max said with his biggest smile? "Not if you get up out of that chair and kiss me."

Max was happy to give in to Dori's affectionate desires any time, any place. After a sweet kiss, they went up to her room, changed into bathing suits and made their way down one flight of stairs to the white sand beach of Sanur and a long row of luxurious wooden lounge chairs with thick white cushions and plush oversized beach towels folded neatly at the end of each chair.

So far, so good Max repeated in his mind. This was not hard to take. The sea in front of them was calm and the water was a delightful 78 degrees. By the time their butts were resting firmly in their seats, a hostess from the bar sidled up to get their drink order. Cappuccinos and cookies were on the way and Max knew it was time to talk, so he started.

"So, here we are," Max said as an ice breaker. Not a great start, he knew. But at least it was something. Dori laughed. "Yes, Max. Here we are. I'm sorry about the dramatic note and then staying here and not calling. I knew you would find out soon enough, but once I got here, I was so wiped out emotionally I didn't want to do anything but sleep. The quiet time last night was really good for me. Now I'm ready for some Max time."

"Are you okay? I read your note more than a few times, and then I talked to the guru. Remission from cancer? Why didn't you say something?"

"I was planning to. I wasn't sure. It might not be anything. I started to feel like I did when I was sick a few years ago. You know, familiar aches and pains and being tired for no reason. I didn't want to get into such heavy shit when there were just a couple more days to be here with you."

"Dori, whatever we do together is making the most out of each day as far as I'm concerned. Thankfully, Wayan was available to drive me, or I would've grabbed a scooter to the airport and ended up in Thailand."

"Ha. That would've been interesting and very endearing. You're a sweet romantic. A woman wants to know the man she loves would do anything to be with her. I'm glad I found you here." Dori leaned in and kissed Max full on the lips.

"I paid for two nights,. Would you like to stay here? I love my room and the bed is super comfortable. And big, she added with a smile and a wink. Let's have dinner and explore a little. What do you think?"

"Sounds great. I like a big bed. Max took a beat waiting for a laugh as if he was on stage at the Comedy Club on Sunset Ave., but got nothing. Dori just shot him a look of acknowledgment. Max continued, but he still thought that was pretty funny. "Sanur is a fun little beach town and it will be cool to check out some different restaurants. I've been eating at the same places here for the last two years."

"Perfect. Something new for both of us. Last one in buys dinner." With that, Dori was up and out of her beach chair and on a fast walk to the water. Max waited a few beats to make sure she got wet first and there would be no argument about who pays.

Dori picked the dinner location after walking up and down each side of the road and a careful review of the curb side menus. She chose a lively cafe with music and al fresco dining. No gas heat lamps needed. And whatever was cooking on the grill, it smelled delicious.

The street scene was like any hip beach town with young people walking past them, holding hands, eating ice cream, laughing and enjoying life. They ate and talked and had a few drinks. Dori had red wine and Max chose the local Bin Tang beer he finally became accustomed to.

Eventually, as inhibitions lowered, they got around to Dori's health. She revealed enough for Max to get the picture while keeping enough to herself to keep things more on the lighthearted side than heavy and depressing.

Dori's doctors detected early signs and symptoms of cervical cancer and were able to treat it without surgery. There was a small tumor which was successfully removed, but she was told that as with any cancer, it wouldn't be uncommon for it to return. Vigilance was key. Hope for the best, be prepared for the rest. "Yada, yada, yada," George said on Seinfeld. Same old bullshit cliches. They stopped for a pistachio gelato on the way back to the hotel, before heading up to their room arm in arm.

Max knew it was a delicate balance and that like for himself, any serious illness is a personal matter and sharing details was the same. He would not press, but he already decided, he would be there in any way she asked or would let him. By the time he got out of the shower, Dori was sleeping soundly on her side facing the moonlit ocean. It was the crescent shape of the new moon. Time for new starts, new chapters. He hung his towel on a hook and eased under the covers next to her. He closed his eyes and let the warmth of their bodies gently touching lull him to sleep.

The morning sun was already bright and pouring in through the curtains Max had opened wide just a few minutes earlier. He was sitting on the balcony with his feet on the railings sipping his room service coffee. His white cotton robe was tied loosely across his waist. "Good morning Mr. Max," Dori said smiling from the bed. She had fun calling him Mr. Max the way the locals did. He turned around happy to see his sweetheart awake and in a good mood. He moved over to the bed and sat down next to her. "Good sleep, he asked?"

"Yes, very good. But I don't feel like getting up just yet. The buffet is open until ten, and I was thinking we could either go to the 8:00 A.M yoga class, or, you know, keep a little busy here. Your call." Max answered by letting his robe fall to the floor and getting back in bed under the covers next to her. Dori put her arms around him, hugging him, kissing him, holding his body tightly against hers.

When she felt him getting aroused, she rolled over on top of him and moved around until their bodies were able to merge together. Once he was inside her, she began to rock gently up and down, backwards and forwards. Max would stop her for a moment when she moved forward, so he could play with her breasts. He would make no excuses for being a breast man. Everyone had legs and a butt. As their passion began to build, their movements became stronger. Max rolled back on top of Dori, and as he thrust into her, she let out a scream. It was not a scream of pleasure and Max rolled off, his face white with worry.

"Dori, what is it? What just happened?"

Dori took a moment to gain her composure and let the pain die down. She knew this pain. It sent her to the doctor in the first place three years ago.

"Max. I had a very small tumor, almost undetectable. It turned out to be cervical cancer. When it's acting up, it's very painful to have sex. It's the last thing I ever wanted to tell you."

"Shit. Dori. Were you in pain the last time we made love? We didn't have to. There's a million,...

"Max. Stop. I didn't say anything, because nothing was bothering me and it's nice feeling normal and doing normal things, like sex. The doctors could hardly find anything to cut out the first time because the tumor was so small. It's probably nothing but a little soreness. I'm feeling better already."

"Well, that's great, but we're going to find out, okay? You can get mad at me later, but I'm calling Wayan for a ride to the clinic.

He lives nearby, and the clinic is around the corner from Om Ham."

"Max. I don't know about going to a clinic here."

"I understand, but I've been there. It's brand new, immaculately clean and well staffed with English speaking doctors and nurses. You will get the best care. I swear."

"Okay. But can we eat first," Dori said flashing a big smile? There are at least five food stations at that buffet I want to try before I leave here."

CHAPTER TWENTY SEVEN

THE CLINIC IN UBUD

Inside the Toyota Ubud Medical Clinic, Max and Wayan waited for Dori to come out of the examination room. She was having blood drawn, X-rays taken and all vitals checked. Max was pacing nervously, thinking back to his experience here. He had been so tired he could barely walk, but kept insisting, just like Dori, that there was nothing wrong. Fortunately for him, a friend at the ashram insisted he go immediately and called for a taxi. It was good that they went. The clinic was more thorough than many of the urgent care centers back home.

They tested for everything, including dengue fever, which is a tropical viral infection spread by mosquitoes. It turned out to be nothing more than a urinary tract infection and the clinic staff brought the meds and all the test results to the hotel in four hours. Then they wanted to take photos with him. Life in Bali. But the point is that he could've died. A urinary tract infection can spread and get into areas that cause sepsis which is often fatal. He kept saying "I'm fine", when in reality he wasn't. If it wasn't for his good friend who called for a taxi and dragged him into it, things could've been a lot different. Finally, Dori was brought out of the exam room by one of the doctors.

Dori had her usual smile and grabbed Max's hand when they were all standing together. She was given a handful of pain pills for the inflammation, and the doctor assured them all the lab results would be rushed over to their hotel by the end of the day. For now, there was nothing to do but relax and be hopeful for good news.

Max and Dori sat under a big umbrella at the pool, and every so often, someone from the Om Ham staff came over to ask her how she was feeling and if there was anything she wanted. Tea, cookies, and coconuts were being brought to their table faster than they could eat them.

"What are you thinking about Dori," Max asked with a bit of fear in his voice as to what the answer might be? As usual, the knot in his stomach was the only fortune teller he needed.

"I called Allie when I was up in my room. I told her to book me a flight and text me the details." "But we didn't even get the lab tests back yet," Max said anxiously.

"I don't need to see them. Whatever the clinic tells us, Max, I know I need to get back and see my doctor. He told me when I left for this trip, to have fun, do what makes me happy, and if anything comes up to get home and take care of it. That's what I'm going to do." Max jumped right in. "I'll come with you."

"No, my sweet man," Dori said with a smile. "I want you right here where I can find you when I come back. Allie lives in my guest house and she's got everything under control. You, on the other hand, have your own tasks at hand, remember? Kirtan, group talks, the harmonium. Need I go on?"
Max was laughing and that's just what Dori wanted.

"Yes, dear. I mean no, dear. No need to go on. I got it. You want me to work while you and Allie party in Los Angeles."

"Exactly. Now, take me to your room and have your way with me. I don't want my last memory of Bali to be from my visit to the Toyota Clinic."

Max was out of his chair leading Dori by the hand to his room for one last night of memories.

CHAPTER TWENTY EIGHT

LIVING LIFE

Dori's departure was hard to accept. Max knew he could have enjoyed living in Los Angeles to be with her. Heck, he lived there for almost forty years without anyone special in his life. But, she was adamant about not wanting him to change the dreams he told her about so often. The last night with her was bitter sweet to say the least. They held hands, slept together with their arms around each other, and said goodbye with a smile and a nod to the future encompassing all plans they discussed. That didn't make it any easier. It took a while for things to settle down with life feeling more like a rollercoaster than a smooth ride on a newly paved highway.

Eventually, the road evened out. Dori sent lots of great, handwritten cards and they spoke live when the hours lined up, laughing and pretending they were lying in bed next to each other. Max was happy that his life started to move forward as he hoped and as Dori hoped for him. That thought made him smile. He knew the less he looked at life through his problems, and the more he concentrated on what made him happy, the lighter his load would feel.

Life is always one ironic twist after another for almost all of us, so it was no surprise to him when he would wake up from a nap or a great meditation and suddenly realize he hadn't talked to the love of his life in a week or sometimes two depending on what she was dealing with.

He would feel a moment of loneliness or sadness when too much time went by without hearing her voice or seeing her lying in bed teasing him and acting like everything was perfect. Everything was far from perfect in his mind, and he wondered what her thoughts were as well during these unintended breaks. When we can't see, feel and touch the person we love, our minds have a way of protecting us and giving us the freedom to find happiness in others. Long distance relationships don't have a history of success. He didn't want that to happen for him, and he hoped it was not happening for Dori.

It would be easy for him, he knew that much. He was always around people and women in his yoga and kirtan groups were always friendly and asking him to have lunch or come over for tea, etc. His greatest worry now, was that something innocent and friendly could turn into something more the longer he was away from his girl. He knew he shouldn't even let these thoughts in and he promised himself he would stop it. His faith in her and love for her told him everything would work out.

Life started to feel seamless once again. The days turned to weeks, and the weeks into months. He was going to kirtan twice a week and getting involved in group discussions that dealt with the spiritual nature of life and all the changes that go with it. He posted on Facebook about a free class he called Max Talks, a take off on the popular events called Ted Talks back in the United States and Europe.

The topic of his talks, The Journey of Love, and the spiritual awakening at its core, was about his personal journey from Los Angeles to Bali and conquering the obstacles that were part of that journey. It was meant to open doors and help others who might feel the same about their life and how much love played a part in it.

The best thing about his talks, was that they kept his heart open and in tune with Dori. Each time someone in the class raised a question on dealing with a lover who lived in another state or country, it gave Max the opportunity to reinforce his own beliefs. Trust what comes from the heart. I am not the body, I am not even the mind.

The night of his first event, he was as nervous as a Jewish teenager minutes before stepping up to the podium to sing his haftorah in front of family and friends. He placed pillows on the floor along the walls and throughout the room, and hoped for at least a few people who would enjoy exploring and expressing their personal and spiritual experiences.

To his surprise, the room was filled with about thirty men and women and the donation basket by the door even had a few bills in it. He turned down the piped in yoga music and introduced himself. In just a few minutes, a great discussion was underway.

Max was a good story- teller who could make his audience laugh while talking about the most serious of topics. Life is funny, he would always say. And the minute you take it too seriously you are doomed. And then he would tell a funny story that helped everyone understand their own unique insignificance compared to the vastness of the universe. Everyone in the room had a story to tell and Max made them all feel safe and happy to share it.

He wanted everyone to understand they are not alone in what happened to them in the past or in what is happening now. An hour later, when his time was up, a few people even stayed to chat with him and ask when his next talk would take place. He noticed with a great feeling of satisfaction, that on their way out, a few people added to his donation basket. That made him feel even better than the kind folks who donated before the class.

On his taxi ride back to Om Ham, he had a feeling of elation that had been missing for a long while. He thought about Dori, and how she gave him the push to do what he truly loved. It wasn't about the money in the donation basket, it was about the love for himself that came from being in that room, talking openly, being free, and speaking from the heart.

Max loved helping people and he had a strong intuitive gift he would share with others when asked for his opinion on something. He had been aware of his psychic gifts for many years and there were many fun aspects to it that made teaching fun for him. When he was teaching 6th grade social studies, if the kids were good all week, he would make the last two hours of every Friday, Psychic Friday.

He would wear a turban, and pick an assistant from the class and tell all the kids who had questions to write them down, roll them up into a ball, and then throw them at his assistant. It was a fun day for everyone. The kids got to throw things, and some of the questions were pretty hilarious. One kid asked if he used a curling iron on his long hair, another asked what kind of pot he smoked. It was anonymous, so they were free to write what they wanted. It wasn't very psychic, but that wasn't the point.

When he walked into his room, he took a hot shower and got into bed. On the nightstand next to him, there was a glass of water with a fresh yellow rose inside. It was resting on the note Dori wrote to him before she left. It was his promise to himself and Dori to keep his room just as she left it that last morning. It was there for motivation, not to dwell on the reasons she left. He told her it would be there when she returns.

Max posted on Facebook again for another Max Talks session, and to his great surprise and gratitude, he had another nearly full room for the event. He made an agreement with Sayuri Healing Foods, the restaurant that used their back studio rooms for such events, to hold his talks every Sunday night at 6:00 P.M and as per usual, the donation basket would be split evenly fifty/fifty between himself and the restaurant. This was one part of his journey that he felt guided to, and thanks to some great friends and intuitive teachers, it was finally underway and going strong.

One of those teachers was the Indonesian healer Wakuha. She was the one who pushed him in the direction he was now headed. Their first meeting was at the Tibetan Bowl healing ceremonies she led every Tuesday and Saturday night at the Yoga Barn. The room was always full, and it was always an amazing night.

He experienced visions and healing that always left him in a far different state of mind than when he first walked in. She would start by sprinkling everyone in the room with holy water from her well. Then in her slow and hypnotic voice she would lead a short deep breathing and Aum chanting followed by the meditation. She always reminded her guests to set their intentions for the meditation. She was a gifted healer and her akashic readings provide a link from the past to the present. She made him realize his true happiness would only come from doing what he truly loved. She convinced him to start his group talks and kirtan and to believe it would work. It would work, she said, because it was what made him happy.

He kept up with his groups and his donation basket provided all he needed for the life he was living just as Wakuha predicted. He felt himself walking tall and smiling from a deep and strong sense of happiness in life. He could tell others around him felt it as well.

People stayed after class to talk. He was invited to tea at people's homes to sit and laugh and share life's experiences. His life was full, and his days were joyful. He talked to Dori whenever the time difference gave them an opportunity. He felt her spirit dancing around him constantly. She was doing well and the radiation and medication was killing all traces of any new infections. They shared sweet dreams of when they would be back together and ended their conversations with love and laughter.

Max was ready for part two of his leap forward. He spent a day with his friend and teacher, Arta, shopping for an harmonium. Arta was an experienced harmonium player and Max loved the sound and wanted to learn how to play the mantras that worked best for singing and chanting in group settings. It was also a good instrument for him to learn. As a young boy around bar mitzvah age, he had become an exceptional accordion player, which is basically the same as a harmonium but is strapped over your chest rather than sitting in a box.

He was never really fond of the accordion, but got stuck with it in high school band class because that was the only instrument left by the time the teacher got to students whose last name started with R. to Z. Ironically, he was really good at playing it. So good that his parents volunteered his services to play at senior centers on weekends. It wasn't his choice for how to spend his weekend mornings, but looking back, he was glad that his parents taught him the value of giving. So now, with his harmonium in front of him, Max was sitting at Arta's side in the yoga classes, learning as an apprentice and being given the opportunity to lead the class in a closing mantra.

Max Talks was doing well enough that he was able to double his time to a two hour commitment at Sayuri. First hour was talk, the second hour was kirtan. Word spread and he kept up with regular Facebook postings, and oftentimes, people from the talk stayed to partake in singing and chanting.

He was no Frank Sinatra, but there were enough good voices singing and pretty faces dancing that no one noticed an out of key note or two. At the end of his most recent kirtan, he was asked by David, a young man with a guitar, from Perth, Australia, if he might play along. Max welcomed the opportunity to add a new sound. And he knew adding a good looking young face would be sure to bring new people to his weekly sessions.

Life found a rhythm, and he was happy. He and Dori continued their FaceTime calls so they could see each other and smile and laugh together. Sometimes, they would listen to music together or do meditation. On some occasions, Max would play his harmonium until she fell asleep. Their bond was strong and their physical distance was not a barrier to their relationship. They made sure not to dwell on her cancer but if something needed to be discussed, it was. There was nothing to hide.

One night on a video chat, Max could see that the day had been a hard one. It was one of the few times Dori didn't ask about his classes or talk about her upcoming visit back to Bali. In a quiet voice just before they hung up, her words hit hard.

"Soulmates don't have to live a whole life together," she said. Their purpose is in finding each other. It can be a week, a day, a year or a lifetime. We will know as we go."

She said that often and with love in her heart and the strength only a woman can be born with. Max knew she was right, and it was his belief as well, but that didn't make hearing it any easier from the woman he loved and waited a lifetime for.

Despite the occasional harsh dose of reality, their relationship seemed to only grow stronger and more compatible. For Max, it was no longer the age old grass is always greener syndrome that posed the occasional problem for him. It was his basic and constant struggle of becoming bored with something once he felt like he had reached a limit with how far it would take him.

No matter how good something was, at some point, he would feel the need for a new and different challenge. One of his friends from L.A. said he had a gypsy's soul and a yogi's heart. He wasn't happy unless he was wandering every so often. It was his Achilles heel.

Thankfully, he was strong enough to keep going and not let Achilles win this battle. As he was putting his song sheets together after a very robust kirtan group and preparing for the night's conversation, a hand went up from the back of the room.

"Max, what are your thoughts on keeping a spiritual connection strong when the physical aspects are impossible due to thousands of miles of distance?" Max took a long look at the woman asking him the question. He had seen her face before, and it was not just in his group sessions. It was from photos Dori had shown him so many times.

"Thank you for that question. Let me give you my best and most hopeful answer. I believe it is one hundred percent possible to keep a strong spiritual connection going regardless of the physical distance between people. There are so many techniques being brought into our yoga and meditation practice these days, that our minds can truly achieve this goal. Lucid dreaming, astral travel, mindfulness, keeping the heart chakra open are all methods we can use to clear our minds and make anything possible. That and simply being honest with each other."
Max's answer led to a lively conversation and many more questions on some of the topics he raised. The group went thirty minutes longer than usual, and finally only one person was left. It was Allie.

"Nice to finally meet you," Max said as Allie got within earshot. Interesting question. "Great answer, Max. Nice to meet you as well."

"You look just like your photos. And you also look a lot like a woman who has been sitting in the back row of my kirtan classes the last two weeks. How long have you been here, he asked?"

"A little over two weeks. Dori asked me to check in on you and check out a few things for her personally. I know I probably should have introduced myself right away, but it was kind of fun being a spy."

"So you've come for your lock of hair?" "Ha. Not really. Something much more interesting. I have a video Dori made for you. How about we meet somewhere tomorrow?"

Max didn't like the idea of waiting, but he agreed to meet Allie at Bodyworks the next morning. She seemed like a good person and it was obvious she had Dori's best interests at heart. He had a restless night, so when he woke, he did the only thing that made any sense to him.

He went to sit at the meditation pond inside the guru's garden at Bodyworks. It was for all the students and staff to enjoy any time and tea was always hot and fresh. It was a place to relax, think and even make friends. He sat there sipping ginger and lemongrass tea and reading over his list of kirtan songs for the next class when he was interrupted.

"Hi, Max. Have you been here long?"

Max looked up to see a beautiful woman with long dark hair and a bright smile walking towards him. She was wearing a white T-shirt with the logo URTH CAFE typed in bold black ink over a graphic of the planet, across the front. It was extra long and covered most of the powder blue runner's shorts she was wearing. He knew the place well.

"Hi Allie. I couldn't sleep so I got here early. The guru and his family live here, and it's become like a second home. Can I pour you a cup of tea?" "Sure. Thank you."

Max got up and poured a cup for Allie and brought it to their table. He had seen a few photos Dori shared with him and heard plenty of stories and now here *she* was while Dori was still back in Los Angeles. Life just isn't fair.

"I don't mean to be impatient, but can I see that video?"

"Absolutely. Can we go somewhere to eat? I walked here and I am starving, Allie replied. It's amazing how you just end up walking and walking and before you know it, you're a few miles from where you started. I could shop on these streets forever."

"Tell me about it," Max replied as he and Allie got up from their seats. He felt the same about shopping and had the t-shirts and shorts to prove it.

Max and Allie went to the All You Can Eat Vegan Veggie Buffet in Ubud Center. Between huge servings of fresh fruits and vegetables, Allie explained that she arrived two weeks earlier and promised Dori she would attend his classes and let her know how he was doing. Max shared his feelings about Dori and how much he missed her.

They ate and talked, and finally full, they paid their bill and walked across the street to Ubud, Aura, where Allie was staying. He had checked it out a few times before deciding on Om Ham, which was a little more suited to his needs. Aura was nice, but the rooms were smaller and there was no pool.

"How do you like this place, Max asked?". "I love it here. I didn't know it was connected to Om Ham until I met one of your friends who works there."

"Let me guess. The tour driver, Sori?"

"Good guess. He told me how much he likes taking you on your adventures. He's quite the ladies man, isn't he? I think he can say hello and what's your number in seven languages."

"Yep. He's a real character. But he's safe. You can trust him and he can show you some great places in Bali that are not on the usual tourist list."

"So, as you noticed, I've been coming to your kirtan and Max Talks classes. I told Dori about them and she is really happy for you and proud of you for taking a chance with your life."

"Thank you, Max answered. I had to. This is as close to a job as I can come. You know, one that doesn't feel like work and doesn't pay enough to buy anything but happiness. And speaking of happiness, when are you going to show me that video?"

"How about right now, Allie said as she pulled her tablet from her purse? Let's sit at the fountain at the Yoga Barn. Is that okay? I love that place."

The fountain at the Yoga Barn was its usual center of activity. It was the easiest to find of all the landmarks in the sprawling city of yoga students, restaurants and living quarters. It provided shade, sunshine and a place to put your feet up and relax. There was even a smoothie bar with vegan chocolate brownies a few hundred feet away. Max and Allie were perched in the shaded end, full lotus pose on display.

Allie flipped her tablet onto its stand and hit play. Max was glued to the screen watching and listening to the message from the woman he fell in love with just a few months ago. Dori looked a little thinner in the face, but otherwise her beauty still took his breath away.

The Video Begins

"Hi Max. I hope Allie didn't tease you for too long before showing you this video. I told her to be gentle with you," she said with a smile and a laugh in her voice. Then she continued.

"I'm feeling so much better and almost at full strength. In fact, your dear Guru has been in touch and has prepared a package of herbs for me that I will collect when I land in Bali. How does next week work for you?"

"Are you kidding," Max asked the screen. Then he turned to Allie. "Is she kidding? Is she coming back?"

"Yes indeed. She didn't want to tell you on the phone and get into too many details that she knew you would ask about. She's so excited to be coming back."

Allie closed her tablet and pulled a sealed envelope from her purse. "This is for you. Dori said you liked letters. I'm not sure what's in it, but I have a pretty good idea. She loves you Max. She probably wouldn't want me to say anything, but she is tired and this trip will not be easy for her. So if you don't want to be on my shit list, think about whatever is in there and don't let her come out here if you're not ready. Got it?"

"Got it. Thanks again, Allie. And for last night as well. It's good to meet you."

"Back at you, Max. I'm glad Dori met such a kind and gentle man. See you in a few days." She gave Max a hug goodbye and walked off to explore Ubud.

Max stayed at the fountain for a while. It was a peaceful place and a quiet retreat from the honking horns of Hanoman street just a block away. He held the envelope in his hand but didn't open it. He wanted to wait until he was back at Om Ham and could swim in the healing waters of the guru's pool and let everything just wash over him. He knew whatever answers he needed would come. All he had to do was let them.

CHAPTER TWENTY NINE

DORI'S VISIT

Max held tight to the letter from Dori as he entered his room at Om Ham. He plopped down on his bed next to the night stand with the fresh yellow rose. It was his constant reminder of the romantic last night they spent together.

There were so many times that he would say he was unlucky in love when asked why he was single. But in his heart, he knew that was not true. He was very lucky in love. The two women he loved the most in his life, until now, had both asked him if he would marry them. The last one being Laurie, the young woman who broke his heart when she told him she loved someone else and had been for the last year of their time together. Someone even older than him, she said, which made him at least laugh a little. He was forty years older than her! At least she was honest in her deceit.

Max still loved her in his memory. Memories were still vivid. They live in our DNA. And how could he forget the night he cooked his famous chicken with turmeric and black pepper and crispy tater tots on the side? As he took the dishes into the kitchen, she called out, "wouldn't it be funny if we got married?" It was kind of funny, considering the forty year age difference, but he would never forget it. Women don't joke about getting married. Especially with the man who is cooking their chicken.

Comfortably resting his back against a few pillows, he gently unsealed the letter and pulled out the light blue paper it was written on. It had angels and hearts all along the borders. This was a good sign, he thought. He began to read silently to himself, but the words were loud and clear.

"Dear Max. I am hoping this short note finds you well and happy. In fact, I hear that is exactly the case according to my dear friend Allie. I'm so glad you met her. She's my closest friend and will be a part of our lives together if all goes well. Let me apologize now for having told her to remain incognito for a little while." There were a few smiley face and heart emojis emphasizing her words. "I wanted to know you were living well and doing the work we talked about together, the things that make you happy. That is what is important to me, Max. That we can be together and do the things that make us strong and happy as individuals and together."

There were a few tears at this point. As long as Dori was in his life, his need for dry eye medication would be greatly reduced. It was like that line from the movie Jerry Maguire, "You had me at hello." He read on…

"I want to tell you how much I have missed you, and how much I have thought about the possibilities that lie ahead for us if we choose to be an *us*. I am feeling better and stronger each day, and I can't wait to be at your next Max Talks class and sing with you in your kirtan group. See you soon, dear Max. Your loving Dori."

Max fell asleep reading Dori's words of love and thinking about what a possible life together would look like. As he slept, the letter moved up and down on his chest with each breath. Morning came quick enough and Max was at the guru's door bright and early. He had things to do and Allie had also asked him to take her to one of the holy water sights for a walk through the water to say prayers and do the cleansing rituals.

He arrived at the ashram earlier than he expected, but that was never a bad thing. The guru saw him and insisted he sit for morning prayers and meditation. He could tell Max was too excited to sit, which is exactly why the guru insisted.

After hearing the news and sharing his thoughts with Max, the guru took his private Om Ham shuttle and drove them to his son's craft shop on Burisma street in the sought after area called Penestanan. It's become a very hip area just about ten minutes from the barrage of passing scooter taxis, yet with the same proximity to ancient temples as Ubud. It's peaceful and quiet and perfect for those who love a little distance from the craziness but like being only five minutes from the latest Italian thin crust pizza joint. The area was rich in beautiful two and three bedroom villas for rent and Max was already thinking this would be the perfect place to live with his sweetheart.

Inside, there were incredible handmade items including sandals, shirts, knives and belts, and rings. The shop owner, Wayan Arsana, one of the guru's five children, pulled out a large tray of rings. They were made from all earth's ingredients. Iron, copper, metal, and silver, and shaped in the images of the many island gods as well as universal symbols and designs.

As the guru and his son described the meaning of each ring, Max let his eyes and heart make the decision for him. He reached for a beautiful copper and coral colored band. Copper for earth and coral for the sea. For himself, Max picked an amber and onyx matte finished band. The guru approved and Max had Dori's ring put on a silver chain until it could be properly placed on her finger.

Max's mind was a little busier than usual. His fairly quiet routine was now one of mixed emotions as he waited for a ride to the airport. He had a few long talks with Allie and really liked her. She was a great friend to Dori and had moved into Dori's house as her full time assistant many years ago. She told Max some great stories and prepared him for the changes he would be sure to notice once Dori was back and sharing his bed.

He knew there would be changes and there were for him as well. He hoped things would pick up from where they left off. Maybe that was a pipe dream or a bit too optimistic, but Max was a dreamer and pipe dreams were right up his alley, so to speak.

The time had finally come. Max was at the airport standing next to the famous customer service desk which was all that separated thousands of just arrived visitors from the crime scene tape like barrier and the way too many taxi drivers on the other side. When he saw Dori walking towards him, still not noticing him, he broke through the line like an alpha dog at the chow line.

"Dori, Dori," he shouted as he waved his hands wildly, like a kid just out of his first day at kindergarten looking for his mom among a sea of moms. Then he saw it. The smile he fell in love with at forty thousand feet above ground. He walked up to his girl and put both arms around her for a hug and then slid his arms down to hold her hand in his.

"Hi Maxie, Dori whispered. How's my favorite guy?"

When Max saw Dori, he didn't notice that her hair was shorter and a bit more grey, and when he held her hand in his, he didn't notice her fingers were not holding his as tight as before. All he noticed was the light in her eyes and the smile that was his to look at forever. He had found his forever. And in the irony of all ironies, it would be a forever that had a built in cloud hanging over it.

As much as Bali is known for being the land of romance, it is also known as the Island of the Gods. There are hundreds of them, scattered all over the island and marked with a temple in every corner. The temples faced the ocean, North, South, East and West, mingling perfectly with the Hindu religion that was practiced by eighty five percent of the population. What better place in the world could there be to rid Dori of the cancer she was carrying?

"Hello beautiful girl. I am so happy to see you. Sori's in his van waiting and Allie is at the ashram getting a few things together for you. Are you ready?"

"Sounds perfect, Max. I'm pretty tired. Can we take a nap together when we get there?" "Can't think of anything better," he answered. Well,… maybe one thing."

Dori smiled as much as her tired eyes would allow and she let her body rest against his shoulder as they walked out of the airport arm in arm and into their future together.

The welcome board at Om Ham was decorated with flowers and WELCOME DORI AND MAX was printed in multi colored chalk across the width. The guru was at the reception desk and came up to greet them with a basket of fruit and coconuts. They were then led to a new room, one of Max's favorites at the resort, 301. It had a huge private balcony and an extra deep bathtub with a separate shower. It was also on the top floor at the very end of the hallway, with views for miles.

"Welcome back Ms. Dori," the guru said as he gave her a warm hug and the keys to her room. Come see me any time and ask at the reception for anything you need. You are our family."

Dori was so happy to be back. She dabbed away a few tears and thanked the guru for everything. Max grabbed her bag and they walked up the stairs to their suite. So many things crossed Max's mind now that Dori had come back to see him. It was one thing to have a short romance and part ways, and it was something else entirely for that short romance to turn into something so much more than he ever would have expected.

One of the things Max would always tell people about being in Ubud, Bali, is that everyone he met seemed to have one thing in common, a strong sense and craving and searching for something that was either missing in their life or something different that would make them happier.

Conversations with complete strangers would start in an instant and last for hours. Divorce, sickness, loneliness, boredom with life, whatever you could think of that made people pack up and look for what in their mind would be better, that had to be better than where they were at. Those were the usual topics of discussion.

Max knew, because he often had those conversations. He hoped he could live happily having what he hoped for instead of wondering if he would ever find it. One thing he knew for sure, he would find out. He did not want to spend another minute of his life searching when what he wanted was right there in front of him with outstretched arms and long brown hair.

As the days passed by, Max and Dori found a simple way to make life work for them. It wasn't hard. Choices were simple. Swimming, exploring new restaurants, bathing in holy water, and of course a little shopping made for a fun menu to choose from.

Max was happy in Bali, and Dori was happy being with Max and having her best friend Allie close by to help her when she needed it. She sang with Max at some of his kirtan groups and made friends with a few of the women who were also from California.

California had become a pretty big expat community and it was always nice to share a little hometown conversation in English. Dori even went to a few of the Max Talks, although she was happy to admit she heard enough of him talking outside of his class. She was mostly fine, but there were days her medication got the best of her. On their good days, they hung out at the pool drinking fresh coconut water and laughing at the craziness that brought them together. They were often seen side by side and if you looked with enough attention, there was always an aura of love and happiness around them that attracted others to just want to sit close and feel their energy.

The guru's herbal medicine bag had been a great help to Dori. In just a few days, her hair had the same luster as when they first met. Her energy was back. The days flew by with hikes through rice fields and day trips to different villages on the island. They got to experience the non-tourist life outside of Ubud.

There were nearby islands Max always wanted to explore, but never being fond of boats on choppy water, he avoided it. Until now. Dori loved the water and that was all the reason he needed. Besides, there were motion sickness pills at every pharmacy. Dori loved all of it, especially the few times she and Max were invited into people's homes and were able to spend time making meals or weaving baskets, playing with children and seeing life that way it is and the way it has been lived for so many years.

They had the most fun in one of Bali's first populated villages, Candidasa, home to the famous Blue Lagoon. Just walking the streets, stopping at the small fruit stands was a trip back in time.

The elderly men and women who had picked the fruits and vegetables from their backyards and had been setting up their little market place for generations, were quick to make sure Max and Dori tasted the ripest mangos and freshest cakes. It was a simple life that still flourished and took care of their families. Max and Dori would hold hands knowing that in their hearts, a simple life together is all that mattered to them. The proof was right there for everyone to see in the smiling happy faces of the Balinese people.

The March full moon was approaching, and Max and the guru were planning a special event at the ashram to celebrate both Max and Dori's union and the full moon. The spiritual meaning of the March full moon, called the worm moon because the worms would appear as the earth got warmer and the time for planting new seeds was perfect. It was also interesting that two days after the full worm moon, the moon is at its closest proximity to earth. It's about love and growth, and any full moon is a time when it fills the universe with its most powerful and magical energies. It was the perfect time to celebrate the union of two people in love.

Max was resting against the steps in the shallow end of the pool, re-reading one of his favorite books- The Alchemist- by Paulo Coelho. He loved this book and had given away many copies to friends as well as people just sitting by the pool who asked him what he was reading. He loved it because it emphasized what was truly important in life.

Life is about the journey, not the destination. Simple words that we have all heard so many times, but words that when taken to heart have the potential to be transformative. Dori walked up behind him and put her hands over his eyes and kissed his neck as she sat down beside him.

"Good morning, Maxie." "Good morning beautiful girl."

This was their official greeting. Max loved it and was so happy and secure that he didn't care who heard it. "Anything going on today or you want to hang out here, Max asked? We can get a massage, sleep, eat, have sex, you know, the basics."

"That's going to be your day for the rest of your life, isn't it?"

"A man can dream, right?"

"Don't stop dreaming, Max. That's one of the things I love most about you. I invited Allie to join us for breakfast. There are a few things I want to tell you about that you have been kind enough not to ask me. And then, I'd like the three of us to spend the day together if that's okay with you."

"Yeah, sure. You get Allie and I'll head over to the dining room. See you all in a minute."

Max, Allie, and Dori ate, drank coffee and sipped on dragon fruit smoothies. They talked for hours. Dori was right that there were things Max did not know yet and was curious about, but the time had come. She explained about her doctor visits in Los Angeles, and that she would not be able to stay as long as she hoped, but as long as the guru's herbs were keeping her strong, she was not going anywhere. She told Max about her home in Los Angeles and that Allie, her best friend since grade school, was living there with her.

They shared stories about their life and dreams and family and friends. They laughed about the stupid things they did in high school and how they managed to get through it all. And most of all, they laughed at how their whole crazy journey led them all to this place, Om Ham, in Ubud, Bali. It was another Bali story and Max knew it would be one he would tell over and over again to anyone who would listen. It was not even that big of a surprise when he learned that Dori had become friends with Fleur and that Fleur and Allie had become a bit of a thing when she made a trip to Los Angeles.

Max was up early the next morning making an extra strong cup of coffee in his room. His thoughts were on Dori and the celebration that would come later that night. A brief moment in front of the mirror told him he was good to go. Hair ruggedly wild, new mala beads around his neck and his favorite two bracelets on his left wrist, the leopard skin jasper and the blood stone that offered him protection and strength. Maybe it was like taking sugar pills without knowing it, but he felt better wearing them all the same.

While he was busy keeping busy, Allie was out taking care of things at the ashram and running a few errands for Dori. Dori had a few surprises planned and it was up to her to make it all happen.

"Knock knock," Dori said in her sing-song voice as she knocked and opened the door." She sounded like Edith from the old Archie Bunker show. This always made Max laugh and he could not get up fast enough to get his arms around her. She had slipped out while he was in the shower and returned with a tray of goodies from the breakfast room. "So, my dear Max, I want to ask you something and I want you to be one hundred percent honest with yourself and with me."

"Okay, Max replied with a bit of hesitation in his voice. Is everything good?"

Dori took his hand and led him to their little bistro table outside the door. They sat down and Max could feel his heart in his stomach. "Everything is great. I am so excited about tonight and being here with you. But there is something I want to ask you now that we have had time to know each other, and know some of each other's frailties. So this is it. Do you really want to live in Bali for the rest of your life?"

Max let out a big exhale. It was a question in his mind since his second trip five years earlier and one that he always played with trying to get to the bottom of. He would ask himself, what if he had a beautiful home and all the resources he needed to live where he liked in the states? Would he still choose Bali twelve months a year?

It's not like Italy or France where everyone speaks English. He would always be a tourist and a stranger in a strange land when you get right down to it. What about doctors and dentists and seeing his two brothers and close friends once in a while? There were plenty of questions to be sure. He took another breath and wrapped both hands around his cup of coffee for something to hold onto.

"Just get right to the heart of things why don't you, Max said, giving himself time to formulate what he would say next."

"It's all right. There is no wrong answer. What's the first thing that comes to you?"

"Well, Dori. I have asked myself that question many times. And now I know the answer. I love it here, that's the truth. And I could live here full time, and that is also the truth. The bigger truth, is that you fell in love with a happy mess, and I rub my eyes every morning I wake up next to you to make sure you're still here and I'm not dreaming. And I could do that anywhere. Anywhere you want. Somewhere warm would be nice. But anywhere you are is where I want to be. Bali is, and always has been, my escape valve. Simple as that. I would live with you in Los Angeles tomorrow if that works best."

"Thank you, Max. I love you for saying all that. It wasn't anything I didn't already know or have a strong suspicion about, and the only thing that matters to me is for you to be happy wherever you choose to be. I always hope that is with me. So, I will tell *you* something now.

My home in Los Angeles is pretty amazing. My dad paid off the mortgage in his will, and left a trust account to cover all the expenses of upkeep, taxes, whatever. I've asked Allie to move into the guest house and when I have to go back to LA, I would like you to come with me. The rest of the time we will live in Ubud near your friends and the ashram. We can figure out the rest as we go. How does that sound?"

Dori let out her own deep sigh and her hands were shaking enough for Max to notice. He took his hands off his coffee mug and put them on top of hers.

"You already have my answer. Wherever you are is where I want to be. It is where I will be. Stalker forever, remember?" They both laughed and when their lips found each other, they backed into their room, fell onto the bed and made love. Max fell asleep in Dori's arms. There were no more words that needed to be said. No more questions that needed to be asked or answered.

CHAPTER THIRTY

THE CEREMONY

Ashram Munivara was lit up like New Orleans at Mardi Gras. Lantern lights hanging from every rafter, and candles everywhere there was a flat surface to put them on. The Guru was dressed in his ceremonial white with a gold band around his sarong, and his altar area was decorated with flowers and surrounded by Tibetan singing bowls.

The staff at Om Ham dressed Max and Dori in the proper wardrobe for their full moon celebration and union as a couple. It was not an official marriage, but for Max and Dori, it was a ceremony to honor their love and promise to each other. Dori's sarong was extra long and flowed beautifully behind her as she walked. She had a white lace blouse adorned by flowers and sandalwood Mala beads the guru himself made for her.

Max was in a dream state watching Dori walk to the entrance of the ashram. He followed along, not really feeling the pavement below his feet. He hoped his mom and dad were smiling down from above.

"Max, hey Max, over here", Allie shouted as he neared Dori's side. Max turned around and was completely taken by surprise when he saw his two brothers and his closest friends standing next to Allie on one side and Fleur on the other. Dori actually became close to Fleur while she was back in Los Angeles getting her radiation treatments. She learned more French and it was no big surprise when Fleur and Allie inhabited her guest house for a few weeks. It was one big happy family and she couldn't wait to see her back in Bali where it all started. The look on Max's face was priceless. She hoped someone snapped a few pics.

"Fuck… are you kidding me. Jeff, Danny, when did you guys get here? Fleur? Mon dieu! What's even happening? This is insane." Max ran over to hug them all. He saved Fleur for last and after a longer hug than the others, he just held her at arm's length for a moment. "You look amazing. Thank you for coming."

"You're welcome, Max. Thank your girlfriend. She paid my way. I'm just a struggling Reiki student. I'm so happy for both of you."

After this sweet greeting, Max noticed Fleur slide over next to Allie and hold her hand. "Why am I not surprised," he asked to no one in particular? "Quiet, Max!" The voices of Allie, Fleur, and Dori rang out as one.

"I can't believe it, Max went on. It's so great you're all here. This is the best surprise. No one has ever visited me here. Now it's a party."

"Well, something had to finally get me here," Jeff said. I'm glad it's your wedding. Congratulations Max. We're all happy for you."

"Thank you. Thank you all. Let's get some photos of all of us together. Honestly, I can't believe you got on a plane for a twenty two hour flight."

"I can't believe it either. And after all that you have us wearing sarongs and funny hats. Where's the bar," Jeff asked with all seriousness?

"All right you guys. We've got twenty minutes to sundown and the guru will start without us. Get a move on," Allie commanded. Pictures and bullshit later!"

The six of them walked into the ashram's prayer circle as one big happy family. They were all seated in the front row, on pillows, of course, and with the sound of a few gongs and Tibetan bowls, the ceremony was under way.

Guru Arsana sang a sacred mantra and his assistants walked around him in a circle, holding candles high in the air. After his mantra, the guru led them all on a slow walk around the Ganesha statue in the center of the fountain three times around. They all chanted either words or sounds and followed the circle around until the guru waved his hands for everyone to sit down. He called Max and Dori to stand next to him, Max on one side, Dori on the other. He said a prayer while holding their hands in his. He then put their hands together in front of him and placed a hand on each of their heads as he recited a prayer and blessing. He closed the ceremony with a simple offering to Ganesha and the prayer that Max and Dori would be forever in a union of love and respect for each other.

Max and Dori said a few words to each other, kissed, exchanged rings and with a loud cheer from the audience, all their friends got up from their pillows and came up to hug and kiss them and embrace their love for each other. Song and dance filled the night and afterwards, Max got photos of Jeff and Danny and his brothers Rich and Ron while they were still dressed in sarongs and sandals. He had to. No one would believe it without proof.

Back at Om Ham, the dining room was kept open for all who wanted to come to share drinks and snacks and give their best wishes to Max and Dori. It was an incredibly beautiful ceremony and Max, Dori, Jeff and Danny drank and ate, sharing laughter and hugs and best wishes.

Fleur and Allie were off in a quiet corner. Fleur arrived a few days ahead of the other guests at Allie's request and their friendship seemed to be blossoming into something more. It was amazing. Max knew right then and there, that if and when it was time to spend a month or two in Los Angeles, that he would have all his closest friends with him.

While Dori and Allie stayed at Om Ham to relax and plan for getting back to Los Angeles, Max spent the next two days with Danny and Jeff, taking them to see a few of his favorite places on the island. His brother's left soon after the ceremony with kids and work waiting for them back home in San Diego. It was a special moment in Max's life and when he dropped his friends at the airport, he knew he was beginning this last crazy part of his life with Dori.

It was something he was missing for so long, he had given up on it. Now, instead of wondering how he could live without love, he was planning on living with his renewed passion for life for as long as he was given. It was a passion that made him promise himself that he wouldn't waste a day of the universe's magic putting them together.

CHAPTER THIRTY ONE

PERDAMAIAN Y CINTA

With Dori and Max's friends back home in California, they each settled into the routine of life Max often dreamed of. He would swim and do yoga and Dori got busy taking Balinese cooking classes with Made's wife along with working on her own yoga program and health routine with the guru. They cooked together, did yoga together and also made sure to do things on their own and keep a strong sense of who they are as individuals and who they are as a couple.

Max kept up with his kirtan groups and before long, Dori was involved with local crafts and keeping a busy schedule of her own. Life was good. They always had breakfast and dinner together and slept holding hands like teenagers in love. They spent some time looking at villas they could rent on a yearly basis. They were really what we in the rest of the world would call houses, but in Bali, rental units are called villas regardless of the size or degree of luxury. They looked in the same neighborhood as Om Ham, just a little north but within walking distance or a short scooter ride. The area was a lush green color year round with scattered villas, restaurants, and rice fields for miles.

Dori was in her element working with various rental agencies. Her father had a vast property portfolio in Los Angeles, and he trained his daughter well. Max had every confidence in her, and was happy to let her do her thing. It was a new experience for him to have enough money in his life that there was no longer any time wasted in making decisions based on what things cost in dollars and cents. It was a good feeling and there were much better things to focus on.

They found a beautiful two bedroom villa with a rosewood front door bordered in turquoise and coral. The door had two sides, and an OM design carved and painted into it above the crescent shaped glass just below the top. It was gorgeous and peaceful and they didn't get fifteen feet into the living space before they asked when they could begin renting.

It only took a few weeks with the help of all their friends from the Ashram, and Max and Dori had a place they called home. They named it Perdamaian y Cinta Villa, House of Peace and Love. It was filled with wicker chairs, leather sofas and a comfortable gel cooled mattress on a wooden platform in each of the two master bedrooms. A beautiful yoga room with windows facing the garden was just off the master bedroom Dori and Max slept in.

The kitchen was stocked with all they needed to make life easy and invite friends over for tea and snacks. The guru and the chef's from Om Ham made sure to fill their kitchen with all the best spices. Of course, the centerpiece was a state of the art coffee machine with a built-in milk frother. Next to that was a four slice toaster, so Max could be sure to start his day with coffee and toast, which was just the way he liked it.

As a Balinese wedding gift, the guru and all his assistants built a beautiful fountain with a small Ganesha statue in the center. It was a mini version of the one at the ashram right down to the small offering plate and incense holders at the base. It was a dream come true for Max. Dori, the love of his life, made it all possible. How things had changed, he said to himself. A few years ago, the love of his life had four legs.

As much as life was rounding into shape, Max was troubled by Dori's escalating bouts of being very tired and sore. The guru's herbs were not working as well as when she first started taking them, and Max knew in his heart that the herbs were not a cure. They were covering her symptoms and helping with the pain.

Dori never complained, but he knew there was a shift somewhere.

"Maxie, Max?" Dori's sweet voice was ringing out. He often didn't answer just so he could hear her call his name again. Ain't love grand. He put down his coffee and looked up at his sweetheart. "Right here beautiful girl. What's up?"

"I was thinking it would be nice to take a drive to the temple at Uluwatu. Are you doing anything today?"

"Nope. Let's do it. I'll gas up the scooter and meet you in the driveway in thirty minutes. Ok?" "Thank you, sweetheart. I'll be out front."

Max loved taking their new scooter for rides. It was a dark blue and white Vespa with extra wide tires for better stability. It was custom made at a specialty scooter shop in Denpasar and they had it fitted with a seat that fit them both comfortably. They added saddlebags for water and food and they were set for any adventure.

He drove a few blocks to the nearest roadside gas station and got what they needed. He still couldn't get over that people used the extra large plastic soda bottles for gasoline containers and sold gas from the front steps of their homes. He had no idea what was really inside those bottles and filled up at a real gas station whenever possible. For now, this would have to do. His sweetheart was waiting.

Max drove back to their villa but Dori was not out front. He waited a few minutes longer and when his beep beep beep went unanswered, he went back inside. He didn't see her and began to call out.

"Dori, hey Dori… where are you?"

There was no answer. Max rushed into their bedroom. Dori's purse was on the bed and the bathroom door was open. Max could see her feet on the floor.

"Dori," he called out as he ran over to her. She was not moving and not awake. He picked her up and placed her gently on the bed with a few pillows under her head. "Dori, can you hear me?"

Max went into the bathroom and ran cold water over a face towel and brought it out to put on Dori's forehead. He kept refreshing the cold water every few minutes and as he was putting the cloth back on her face, she sat up just a little. "Hi Maxie. Do you believe in angels," she whispered with all the smile she could muster?

"Of course I do beautiful girl. I am holding one's hand right now. What's going on here? Can I get you anything?"

"Water please," Dori whispered.

Max filled a glass and put it next to her. "I'm going to the ashram to get the guru. Will you be okay? I'll be right back. Two minutes."

"I'm fine. It would be nice to see him."

As Max and the guru rode back to his villa he explained what happened. The guru just nodded as if he had an understanding that went deeper than anything he could explain. Max wondered what Dori was getting at when she mentioned angels, but when he opened the door to their bedroom, he saw what looked like an hourglass shaped white cloud drifting above Dori's head. It hovered a bit and then floated out through the skylight over their bed.

"Guru is here sweetheart. Can he come in now?"

Dori nodded and took Max's hand in hers. I love you my dear Max. Will you do me a favor?"

"Of course. Anything," Max assured her." "Will you write our story, and live in our villa?"

"That's two favors," Max said, trying to be brave.

"Promise me, Max." "I promise."

Max leaned in and kissed Dori on the lips, softly, with all the love in his heart until her lips closed. She opened her eyes.

"I'm your angel, dear Max and you were mine." Then her eyes closed.

"Guru, can you come in please," Max called out.

The guru came in and he motioned for Max to go out of the room. He put one hand on Dori's stomach and one hand on her head and breathed all the power of his heart's energy into her. Her eyes didn't open and the guru knew she had passed. Her life force was gone and with her last breath she felt Max's love flow into her soul.

Max was sitting by the Ganesh fountain the guru and his friends built for their villa. His elbows were on his knees and his forehead was bent forward into his hands. As quickly as he could wipe away his tears, they were flowing again. He couldn't form words if he wanted to. The guru sat down next to him and as much as Max loved this man and the wisdom he offered, he didn't want any part of it at this moment. The guru just rested his hands on Max's head for a moment and told him gently to stay here in Ubud. Now was not the time for him to leave. He got up and when he got to the driveway he turned back to Max.

"Stay here, Max. Dori picked this villa for you. She told me her dream many times and what she wanted most was for you to be happy in the place you loved."

CHAPTER THIRTY TWO

DUST TO DUST

Allie was back in Ubud, and all the arrangements had been made through the hospital in Denpasar. She had many talks with Dori about what to do when her time had come. It was a hard few days with Max, and as much as she wanted to help him, there was nothing she could do. She left him the five year lease on the villa that Dori had taken care of and she gave him keys to their home in Los Angeles. Dori put Max's name on the deed with Allie's and Allie told him he was welcome any time for as long as he wanted. They were family now and would honor Dori's wishes to keep their home filled with love and great memories.

Allie flew back to Los Angeles with Dori's body so that family and friend's could say good-bye. She told Max that Dori hoped he would understand, but she wanted him to stay in Ubud. She knew it would not be healthy for him to come back for something he already dealt with at their villa.

The days were long and difficult for Max. He went back to his room at Om Ham to take a break from the villa. He posted on his Facebook page about Dori's passing, and that Max Talks and his kirtan groups would be taking time off. He was not in his room very often and when the guru came by to look for him, Govinda at the reception desk told him that Max took his things from their room and didn't want to stay there another night. He went somewhere with Sori from transportation and didn't leave word.

There was no point in trying to keep anything from the Guru, so it was no surprise that he found Max in that small village of Candidasa he visited with Dori. They had an amazing romantic weekend there at the luxury resort Alila, and outside of the ashram and their own villa, it was her favorite place on the island. When he was told the room they were in on their previous visit was available, he booked it for a few days. The guru rang his room from the registration desk and when there was no answer, he walked to the private beach in the back of the hotel.

Alila was a luxury resort and the beach was private and beautiful with views all the way to the other side where the famous Blue Lagoon was filmed. Max was sitting at the water's edge letting the waves wash over his feet. The guru walked up behind him.

"What are you doing here Max?" Max turned around but he knew it was the guru from the sound of his voice.

"I told Sori not to tell anyone where I was."

"I think you should come back with me, Max. Your friends and family are at the ashram. We are all here to help in any way."

"I understand," Max replied. "I am so thankful and grateful to all of you. For now, I need a little time to myself. I'll be back in a couple of days. I promise."

"All right, Mr. Max. Come to Bodyworks when you get home."

"Thank you, guru, for coming all this way. I will be there." Max could barely look the guru in the eyes and the guru understood. He left him at the beach with the hope he would see him soon.

Max kept true to his word, and after a couple of days of sleeping in the bed he and Dori shared just weeks earlier, he showed up at the guru's healing center. The Guru took him to where his master lived. It was farther north in Bali at a very big ashram with a huge waterfall and sacred pool with a meditation area.

The guru led him through the various temples, the rooms for silent meditation only, and bathing in the holy water. Lastly, the guru worked on his body for almost two hours, digging deep to push the emotional pain out of his body. He was in an altered state for sure and the Guru drove him to his villa to rest and sleep. He told Max to just be still and let the work he just experienced take hold. The staff would bring him fresh fruits and tea. Max nodded in agreement and thanks and walked through the gorgeous wooden doors to the bedroom in his villa.

The Guru's work knocked him out and he slept about sixteen hours into the next day. He moved around under the covers, letting his body stretch and wake up on its own timetable. There was no rush for anything anymore in his mind. He peeled back the lace curtains and realized that the morning fog had already burned off and the sun was beginning to warm things up. The birds were singing so he had to move a little closer to the front door to check what he thought were his wind chimes making a familiar sound.

When he walked out to the front of his villa he was greeted by a familiar but unexpected sight. Standing out front by the fountain, the staff and many of the people from his kirtan group were waiting. They set up a long table of food and drinks and Arta was playing his harmonium. A few of Dori's new friends came up and gave Max a big hug and sweet kisses and offered their kindness to help him with anything he needed. It was a beautiful day of sharing stories, food and laughter. Not a soul there would let Max feel alone.

By nightfall, long after the last guest had departed, he was sitting alone with Lea. They talked a bit and sat silent together unaware of the time and with no regard for it. He didn't want to move and she was in no hurry to leave. Lea was a dazzling beauty with long, curly auburn hair and a lithe sculpted body formed by years of doing and teaching dance and yoga.

She was from Perth, Australia, and she and Dori became fast friends during kirtan groups and fun side trips for lunch and shopping. They shared similar stories of how they came to be living in Bali and developed a kinship of sorts. Lea was about Dori's age with a gentle spirit and soft smile. Dori told her how much she wanted to visit Perth one day, and New Zealand and they had put it down as something they would do together soon.

All the things we say we will do "One Day", Max told himself. One day is a dangerous place to live. Lea told him the group hoped he would come back soon and that he was loved and missed. She also told him that on a personal level, she hoped he would come back or at least call her if he felt alone and wanted some company. It wasn't anything more than a gentle nudge to a man she felt safe and comfortable with as well as a certain affinity for after all the yoga and kirtan they shared. And with that sweet goodbye, she hopped on her scooter and drove down the driveway to her own home on the island.

Max knew he was a changed man. His eyes followed her until her scooter turned the corner of the long driveway on the busy street of Tirta Tawar. He was happy for the company, and thankful for the affection from Lea. He had no thoughts about calling her or anyone at the moment. He was back to being alone and had to make sense of that all over again. Love conquered all just as he always suspected, but will that one true love keep his heart filled and mind at peace for all the days ahead of him? Was he ready to move forward with all the beauty of life the universe offers to those who are ready to accept it? Time would tell was all he could think of in answer to that question.

CHAPTER THIRTY THREE

THE CIRCLE OF LIFE

It was three months after Dori's and Max's celebration at the ashram. That's how Max thought of time these days. From the date of their union, not the date of her passing. His hair was quite long now, well past his shoulders. It would most likely continue to grow without Dori's teasing about him looking like a backpacker who was lost in the mountains for a year. It reminded him of the day he stopped at a roadside restaurant with his friend Joana.

They were on the way back to Om Ham from one of the nearby waterfalls, when the urge for French fries came over both of them. While they were standing at the cashier's desk, the two young Balinese girls working the counter started giggling. Max asked them what they were laughing about. One of the girls smiled and said so politely to him, "You look like Albert Einstein." Max and JoAna started laughing with them. Max was not upset at all. Quite the opposite. He felt good to know these young women knew who Albert Einstein was in the first place. He also did look a bit like the old wizard of time and space.

Rainy season had begun and it was a good time to have things to do indoors. Max was sitting at his writer's desk, alternating between staring at his computer screen and the gorgeous view out of his bedroom window of the heavy rain pouring down sideways while slamming into everything in its path. It was the perfect soundtrack for the task at hand. Dori loved the rain in Bali. There was never much of it to experience in California, so she would just sit outside at their table underneath the big umbrella and listen and watch in awe of good old mother nature. And she loved making love to the sound of the rain. She loved love and Max knew for once in his life, he had the love of the only woman he ever loved. Why couldn't it last as long as the crappy relationships he had, he wanted to ask someone.

He sat at his desk often, but that's all he did. He would sit and look out the window. He wanted to write the story Dori asked him to write, he was just having a hard time getting started. He walked out back to the table Dori used to sit at while listening to the rain. WHAM! A loud crackle of thunder shook the ground and a bright bolt of lightning struck near the coconut palm tree a few yards away. Okay, he said to the clouds above. Thinking of her and the promise he made, he was motivated enough to begin.

He was smiling now as he remembered that it took an extra bit of magic to get his fingers moving on his computer. He had gone into the kitchen to make an extra strong cup of coffee and when he walked back towards his desk, he saw a familiar white cloud dancing above his screen. It just hung there, shapeless, dancing, until it waved goodbye and floated through the window.

"Okay Dori, I get it," Max said to his angel. He sat down with a renewed passion and as his fingers hit the keyboard a loud clap of thunder followed by a brilliant streak of lightning shook the window sill and lit up the fountain. With that, Max was back to work. He found the love of his life. Life was complete in that sense, but far from over. He was ready for what lies ahead.

And for those who would deny such supernatural events, Max asks you to explain the occasional heart shape drawings he would find traced into his foggy windows after a rainy night.

Sitting at his computer, Max begin to write the story he promised Dori he will tell. It's the story of their love and the home Dori built for them in Ubud, Bali. Their home was named the House of Peace and Love and Max used that as the title for his screenplay.

FADE IN:

DARK CLOUDS AND A RAIN FILLED SKY SOAKED THE TARMAC AT LOS ANGELES INTERNATIONAL AIRPORT

INT. DAY - TERMINAL FOR CHINA AIRLINES

Max makes his way to the boarding gate for his twenty one hour flight to Bali. He is alone but not unnoticed…

TWO YEARS LATER

Two years later, Max and Allie were standing anxiously in front of a Barnes and Nobles book store in Los Angeles. There was a big poster of Max and Dori and he and Allie were standing nearby in front of a table filled with hardcover copies of his book. His novel was written as a screenplay and made into a feature film.

Max had settled into the guest house on a part time basis once he finished writing his novel. He was happy to have such a great place with friends and family nearby for the few months a year he was back in LA. The rest of the year, he was most happy back at the villa he and Dori made a life in. It was filled with happy memories and surrounded with enough buddha and angel statues to invite all sorts of heavenly spirits. Dori was never far from his thoughts, and when he needed it most, a beautiful angelic cloud would come by for a visit. Or trace a heart in a foggy window.

Allie lived in the main house most of the year and would come visit Max in Bali whenever she had a couple of months to truly enjoy it. Fleur would visit her in Los Angeles and stay with her for a month at a time and then head back to her studies in Paris. Sometimes, she would join Allie in Bali and she was welcome and part of their family. They all shared love and laughter and great stories.

Lea became a regular guest, joining Max for dinner and an occasional night together. Their relationship was simple. They would take turns cooking and going out to try new restaurants. Whenever she wanted a good laugh, she would try and teach Max the joy of ecstatic dance. Other times, they were content to sit together holding hands and occasionally sleep next to each other as friends comforting each other. Over time, Lea got to know Allie and Fleur and the four of them kept love alive in the villa of peace and love. Life is good.

THE END

GLOSSARY

Om Ham Retreat and Resort - Jalan Tirta Tawar, Ubud.
Gianyar Bali. 80571   +62 361-9000-352

Bali Pure - organic fruits, smoothies, drinks, snacks, Tirta Tawar
80571.   +62 821-3964-7518

Muse Cafe and Art - Ji Sri Wedari No.6b Ubud 80571
+62 811-3809-394 - Digital Nomad heaven

Pyramids of Chi - Jalan Kelebang Moding Nol 22 Ubud 80571
+62 821-4782-3397

*****ZEST Vegan/veg Restaurant - +62 823-4006-5048
Ji. Penestanan Kelod Ji. No. 8 Sayan Gianyar, Bali 80571
Across from Tony Blanco art Museum- Digital Nomads welcome

****SAYURI Healing Food-Vegan chocolate +62 822-4048-5154
JI.Sukma Kesuma no.2 Peliatan Gianyar, 80571 Ubud Center
Amazing. Digital Nomads, kirtan groups, best food ever

Pura Tirta Empul - Holy Water Springs, Cleansing w/guide
Ji.Tirta, Manukaya, Kec. Gianyar, Bali 80552 Hindu Temple

**** Master Ketut Arsana's Bodyworks Healing Center - Ubud
JI. Hanoman St. No. 25 Ubud Gianyar, Bali 80571
+62 361-971393

www.wakuha.com -meditation teacher, intuitive healer, sound
healing weekly at www.theyogabarn.com

Monsieur Spoon - Delicious bakery/digital nomad space, fresh
oven baked croissants, cookies, pastries, more.
99 JI Hanoman #10 Ubud, Bali, near Yoga Barn, Monkey Forest